BOOKS BY

JOHN SWARTZWELDER

THE TIME MACHINE DID IT (2004)

DOUBLE WONDERFUL (2005)

HOW I CONQUERED YOUR PLANET (2006)

THE EXPLODING DETECTIVE (2007)

DEAD MEN SCARE ME STUPID (2008)

EARTH VS. EVERYBODY (2009)

THE LAST DETECTIVE ALIVE (2010)

THE LAST DETECTIVE ALIVE

JOHN SWARTZWELDER

Kennydale Books
Chatsworth, California

Published by:
Kennydale Books
P.O. Box 3925
Chatsworth, California 91313-3925

First Printing April, 2010

ISBN 13 (paperback edition) 978-0-9822736-2-3
ISBN 13 (hardback edition) 978-0-9822736-3-0
ISBN 10 (paperback edition) 0-9822736-2-2
ISBN 10 (hardback edition) 0-9822736-3-0

Library of Congress Control Number: 2010902570

Printed in the United States of America

CHAPTER ONE

"**L**et's pull the plug on him," I heard a voice say. "It looks like he's coming out of it," said an older, calmer, voice.

"Let's pull the plug on him," insisted the first voice, jangling the keys in his pockets restlessly. "Let's pull the plug on everybody."

"Take it easy, Bobby."

"Doctor Bobby."

"Okay, Doctor Bobby. But slow down. This is just your first day. You've got to learn to pace yourself."

"I'm going to go amputate somebody's leg."

As the young doctor hurried out of the room, I opened my eyes and looked around blearily. A kindly looking old doctor was next to my bed, looking down at me.

I made an effort to speak: "When I came in here..." I said, "...I had a sandwich."

"That was three months ago," said the doctor.

I looked at him.

"It's gone," he said, gently.

1

I lapsed back into unconsciousness.

I was in the trauma ward of Central City Hospital, and had been in a coma for several months, they told me. I was in pretty bad shape. They said I had pulled every muscle in my body, including that big muscle you have in your brain that thinks about sports, and the muscle that wags your vestigial tail when you see a friend. I asked if I had broken the record for pulled muscles, but they said they didn't keep records like that anymore. It attracted the wrong kind of people to the medical field—the gambling element. Anyway, I bet I broke the record, whatever it was. I'll bet a hundred dollars on that.

The doctors asked me how I had gotten myself banged up so badly in just one lifetime. They didn't believe it was possible. I told them the important thing was you had to start young. I started telling them the whole story, beginning with my botched conception, then moving on to my explosive delivery and my near fatal first attempts to put my foot in my mouth. At that point they told me they were more interested in the cause of my current injuries, and that I should skip on down to that. So I told them about what had happened to me this year.

I had been chasing after a con man named Edward Blinkman, or "Blinky", as he was called, because he blinked his eyes all the time, I guess. And hey, his last name is "Blink-Man". I never noticed that before. Anyway, he had conned my client, Mr. Aristotle Acropolis, out of a fortune, talking him into buying a bunch of "historical collectibles" at fantastic prices that were neither historical nor collectible. The only thing that was true about the whole thing was the fantastic price. Acropolis knew nothing of history, but he was greedy, so he was an easy mark for Blinky, who didn't know anything about history either, but was greedier.

Blinky brokered deals between Acropolis and a group of recently paroled autograph dealers, with the result that Acropolis now had the largest collection of totally unknown Revolutionary War signatures in the world: Nathanial Pillman, Tad Gump, General Oddsbody, the officers and men of Pickle's Rangers, and President Snodwell, to name but a few of the more expensive ones.

It was only after Blinky and his accomplices had cashed the check and gotten well away, and were having a loud party in a neighboring state that you could hear in this state, even with your windows closed, that Acropolis got around to showing some of his prize autographs to members of his club. That's when he found out the shocking truth. There was no President Snodwell. Roderick Snodwell, despite his flamboyant signature, was nothing more than a Revolutionary Era grocer. Nathanial Pillman wasn't famous either. He worked for Snodwell, bagging groceries. Tad Gump's autograph hadn't been worth a penny when he originally wrote it and it had been going down in value for hundreds of years now, with no bottom in sight.

When he found out he'd been cheated, Acropolis was furious, but he refused to call in the police. Getting the police involved would result in publicity, he knew, and he didn't want any publicity about this. If word of how he'd been duped ever got out he would be a laughingstock in society again, as he was in '59 and '72. He wanted this done discretely, like it was done in '64, '83, and last year. So he hired me to find Blinky and make him return the money and take his valueless autographs back, as discretely as possible. I told Acropolis the case was as good as solved. I knew I was safe in saying this because the old guy obviously believed everything anybody told him.

My investigation into the case started slow, as my investigations always do. I have a technique for looking for people. Some say it's lazy, but I prefer to describe it as methodical. It's probably a little of both, I guess.

First I look around in the room I'm in. It will save me a lot of time and legwork if the man I'm looking for is standing right in front of me, with his hands up. If there's a box in the room, I'll open it. He might be in the box. In the event of multiple boxes, I start with the nearest box. That way I don't have to get out of my chair right away. I also open a lot of drawers. You'd be surprised at how many criminals hide in drawers. And probably equally surprised at how many who don't. But you have to actually open the drawers before you'll know which way this case is going.

After I'm pretty sure he's not hiding anywhere in my house, I hit the streets. Maybe he's standing out on the street. Maybe in front of my building. Probably with his hands up. If he's not, I start asking around and showing people his picture.

After I'd shown Blinky his own picture on five separate occasions, somebody tapped me on the shoulder and said: "Hey, there's the guy you're looking for." And I said: "Where?" And he said: "You're talking to him, stupid."

I lunged. Blinky threw the picture in my face, momentarily blinding and disorienting me, and escaped in the confusion.

I cornered him a little ways down the street at a gas station, where he was pausing to get a getaway map. I chased him around the office, with first him, then both of us, taking money out of the cash register as we ran, while the gas station owner looked on in horror. It was while I was pausing to see if there was any money in the safe that Blinky made his escape.

Over the next four months, I chased him from continent to continent, over mountains, across prairies, over cliffs, everywhere. I chased him across a tightrope at the circus—we both got a big hand for that—chased him through some woman's bedroom, who now has a child that looks like both of us, and chased him over Niagara Falls in separate barrels. Sometimes we were thousands of miles apart. Sometimes we were much closer. Like when we were briefly seated at the same table at a restaurant. Or when we found ourselves kissing each other in a dark theater. But no matter how close I got, I never quite managed to catch him. He always got away from me again somehow.

Every time I tracked him down again I found him working some new scam on some new unsuspecting sucker—selling rare books that weren't rare, "antiques" that were really "new things", and so on. He even conned me out of some money a few times. I don't know why I bought the Brooklyn Bridge twice. I mean, I already owned it, right? Why do I have to buy it again? Somebody explain that to me.

It usually took me quite awhile after I realized I had been conned to realize that I had been conned by the man I was looking for. That's a complicated thought, involving, as it does, a combination of two different, but closely related, thoughts, so it usually took me awhile. It was made harder by the fact that I hardly ever recognized Blinky. His disguises always fooled me, even though they were usually pretty rudimentary—sometimes just a false mustache, or a toothpick. Sometimes he would just stick out his tongue or close one eye, or just turn around. But no matter how simple his disguise was, it was always enough to make him look like a completely different person to me.

I tried wearing a disguise myself for awhile during our chase, since disguises seemed to be so effective, but it didn't help me find him, and now I didn't know who I was either. I finally took off the disguise. I was confused enough as it was. No point in making it worse.

My relentless pursuit of Blinky was kind of like a real life version of that TV show "The Fugitive". Remember that one? David Janssen played the bad guy—the guy who kept running when everybody wanted him to stop. I watched tapes of the show regularly during our chase, hoping to get some fugitive chasing tips, and always yelling: "Get him! Get him!" to Lt. Gerard. But he never did. And I never caught my fugitive either.

It was our trip over Niagara Falls—my barrel, complete with siren, chasing his barrel—and the subsequent bouncing of my barrel out of the river, down the freeway, and into the middle of that Grand Championship Demolition Derby And Pile-Driver Exhibition, that finally ended the chase, landed me in the hospital, and put me in this coma you've been reading about.

When I finished telling all this to the doctors, I noticed they were gone. Apparently they had been gone for a long time. Just cobwebs there now. So the next time they asked me how I had managed to get myself all banged up like this, I just said I didn't know.

I was in a hurry to get well and get out of the hospital, partly because I wanted to get back to the chase, but mostly because I don't like being in hospitals. They feed you through a tube, for one thing. I kept telling them I was well enough to be fed through a hose, but they said I wasn't that well yet. Well then, I said, how about putting the tube in my mouth, where food goes, instead of the stupid place you've been putting it? For doctors, you guys sure don't know much about the human body. They said be quiet now.

I also don't like the hospital gowns they make you wear. There's something undignified about having no back to your pants. When it comes to pants, the back is one of the things you want most. The gown I had to wear was drafty, undignified, and a terrible temptation to practical jokers. I don't want to go into a lot of detail here about this, but I'd like to know who has been supplying the hospital patients with firecrackers.

When the doctors decided I was more or less recovered, and had determined that they had gotten as much out of my insurance company—Ed's Insurance—as they were ever going to get (Ed had shot himself), they released me.

I walked slowly and still a little painfully out of the hospital, trying to decide if I should get back on Blinky's trail right away or maybe wait until I stopped seeing three hundred of everything.

It was while I was brooding about my imperfect physical condition, and all the bad things that had happened to me recently, and thinking about how hard it was to be me, and wishing that I wasn't me, oh why oh why was I me?, that I suddenly discovered that I wasn't me anymore. Some other guy was.

"You can't push Frank Burly around!" I heard

a squeaky voice shouting. "Frank Burly defies you!"

"Hey, listen, Burly…" said another voice.

I looked across the street. A bunch of irate people were crowded around a smaller man I couldn't quite see.

"Go ahead and ruin my credit, Mr. Businessman!" the squeaky voice continued defiantly. "Give me all the god damn tickets you want, Mr. Policeman! Frank Burly doesn't care!"

"Well, I think I will ruin your credit," said the businessman.

"Good!"

"And, because of your insolence," said the policeman, "I'm going to give you another ticket."

"Fine!"

"Hey!" I yelled, urgently pushing my drip-stand towards this confrontation. (The hospital had forgotten to disconnect me from my drip-stand.) "What's going on over there? He's not Frank Burly! I am!"

I pushed my way through the crowd and came face to face with a small pugnacious man who was wearing my hat and tearing up my tickets. It was Blinky.

"You!" I roared.

He took off and began running down the street, with me on his heels, bellowing with a mixture of rage and triumph. This wasn't the closest I had gotten to my quarry over the course of our long chase—the previous Halloween I had unwittingly worn him as a mask—but it was the closest I'd gotten in months.

Even with the drip-stand slowing my progress, and everyone laughing at me because I had no pants (the hospital had released me without pants), I was making pretty good time and had nearly caught up to Blinky when he suddenly vanished into thin air. One second he was running down the sidewalk and thumbing his crooked nose at me, the next he was gone.

I looked around the area for awhile, but found nothing. A crowd of people had gathered to look at my ass, so I took the opportunity to ask them if they had seen where Blinky had gone. They hadn't. They said they could see my ass though. I said I wasn't looking for that. I knew where that was. Everybody did now.

I took one more slow and careful look around, giving everybody one last panoramic view of my ass, then I gave up the search and went home.

CHAPTER TWO

On my way home I figured I'd better stop and get some money. The doctors hadn't found a wallet on me when I was brought into the hospital, though they had looked for hours, so I guessed it hadn't survived the trip over Niagara Falls. Or maybe it had been taken to a different hospital. Anyway, I needed some cash.

I stopped in at my bank and tried to take some money out, but they said there wasn't any money in the account. It had all been withdrawn. And anyway, it wasn't my account. Because I wasn't Frank Burly. I said yes I was. They said no I wasn't. I kept saying yes I was for quite awhile, but they kept replying no I wasn't. It was the nearest thing to a stalemate I had ever seen.

"You have no identification to prove you're Frank Burly," the bank manager pointed out.

"There's a funny story connected with my lack of identification," I said.

The bank manager interrupted my laughter. "Whereas the real Frank Burly, who removed all the money from this account several days ago, does."

"Huh?"

"And, just for your information, Mr. Phony..."

"Burly," I said, correcting his pronunciation. I don't know why so many people get that wrong.

"...the real Frank Burly wears a snap-brim fedora, not a pork pie hat. Next time you're trying to impersonate somebody, find out what kind of a hat he wears. That's my advice to you."

"Somebody stole my hat and left this in its place."

"Hmm..." the bank manager said, thoughtfully. "A clever story. In fact, it's fantastically clever. But the fact remains that you have no account here."

"Yes I do."

Which started us on a whole new argument that took up most of the rest of the afternoon, before it finally concluded with the words: "No you don't" and "Yes I do".

When I got home I found someone had been living in my house and sleeping in my bed. I felt like The Three Bears. I checked the kitchen. Sure enough, all my porridge was gone. It was easy enough to figure out who the intruder was. He had made the classic mistake so many beginning criminals make of taking down all the pictures of me in the house and putting up pictures of him. It was Blinky. He had apparently been living in my house all the time I'd been cooped up in the hospital. There wasn't a clean dish or empty ashtray in the house. And he'd converted my garage into a rec room. That made me mad. I felt I should have been consulted first on that.

He'd been using my office too, posing as me, and doing his best, apparently, to ruin my professional reputation. There were all kinds of angry messages on my answering machine from clients I'd never heard of, saying they had paid me, but that I had never done the work. My desk was piled high with bills, dun notices from credit card companies, traffic tickets, subpoenas, and official notices informing me that my driver's license had been suspended, my private detective's license had been revoked, my credit rating had reached zero, and I was under arrest.

Cursing Blinky, I swept the bills and the answering machine into the trash and called up the Police Commissioner. Getting my investigator's license back was the most important thing, so I'd fix that problem first. I told the Commissioner what had happened, as briefly and as concisely as possible, only using such sound effects as seemed necessary. When I was finished he made his own sound effect, and said he didn't believe a word of it. It was just too far-fetched. He reminded me that he wasn't born yesterday. I asked when he was born. I would like to send him a present. An expensive present, if he knew what I meant. He said goodbye. I said goodbye, Bill. He said not to call him Bill.

Then I called up the credit card companies.

They weren't born yesterday either. I guess nobody was.

I had always laughed at victims of identity theft before this. I don't know what seemed so funny about it to me. It just made me laugh, that's all. I thought victims of identity theft were a riot. But I wasn't laughing now. This was serious.

Not only was Blinky racking up enormous bills in my name and trashing my reputation, now I couldn't do it. He had all my identification, so I couldn't prove who I was anymore. It's annoying enough to be without ID in normal times, but these were not normal times.

Because of heightened security concerns in Central City (only last week a terrorist had punched the Mayor in the face), there were strict new rules in place to discourage terrorism. You needed to show your ID now to enter public buildings, use the crosswalks, open an umbrella, or flush your toilet. Under the new rules, the man who had punched the Mayor would need at least three pieces of ID to do it again. And you had to show 5 pieces of ID to blow up a plane, and 20 pieces of ID to take over the Government. That would certainly discourage the terrorists, everyone felt. Just think of all the lines they will have to stand in! They'll be there all day! On the other hand, if you didn't have any valid form of identification at all, like me, the only thing you could do was vote.

I decided that the first thing I should do was find Blinky and get my ID back, and stop him before he got me into even more trouble than he already had. Then I could figure out how to sort out the rest of this mess. But finding people takes time and money. And I was broke. Fortunately, I knew where I could get all the money I wanted—from my gullible and insanely wealthy client, Aristotle Acropolis.

Acropolis had a mammoth mansion on the biggest and snootiest hill in Central City. His lawn was the size of a football field. His driveway was part of the interstate freeway system—a main part. You couldn't drive from New York to Los Angeles without going through his garage. His front door was the size of a battleship. His servants were as big as trees. He had a big place, that's the point I'm trying to get across here. I was going to exaggerate the size of his place, but I decided I didn't have to.

I was ushered into his opera-house-sized study by his gigantic butler. Acropolis was sitting in his monstrous chair, peering over the edge of his preposterous desk. His telephone was as big as a motorcycle. His paperclips were the size of mountain lions. Having all this big stuff around him made him look important, which I guess was the look he was going for, but it also made him look like the Incredible Shrinking Millionaire.

"Well?" he demanded, when I came in.

"I lost him," I said. I tried to sound proud.

"You what?" he roared.

I made a little motion with my hand to indicate that there was more to the story than just me screwing up. Much more. And that if he would just reserve his judgment until he heard the whole story, he...

"Stop waving your hands around and say something!" he snapped.

"Yes sir."

I quickly launched into a complete report of all that had happened since he had hired me the year before. I sanitized this report as much as I could, because I planned to conclude it by asking him for more money. So I tried to make it sound like I had done a pretty good job overall, when you thought about it, and that all of my decisions along the way had been the right ones, more or less, and that every time I lost Blinky it had been a stroke of genius, and that far from being criticized for the way I had handled the case so far, I should be given a parade.

It had all sounded great when I rehearsed it in the bathroom that morning, when I only had to convince myself, but it sounded pretty lame now, even to me. By the time I was nearing the end of my report, both of us were kind of sneering at it. I wasn't even bothering to finish a lot of my sentences. Who cares, anyway? Not fooling anybody.

"And the minute I got out of that coma and lost him again, I reported back here to you," I concluded, listlessly. "Blah blah blah, bullshit bullshit."

Acropolis snorted derisively. "And you call yourself a detective!"

"Well… sometimes I do."

"I hope you have your fingers crossed when you call yourself a detective."

"Yeah, I usually cross 'em. Now if you could just advance me a little more expense money…"

"You'll get no more money from me until you've found the man I've hired you to find." He looked at the new hat I was wearing. "I'd better not see that hat on your expense account."

"You won't see it."

"Good."

"It'll be on the back."

"Take it off the bill entirely."

"Yes sir," I said obediently. It doesn't pay to argue with a client. I would put the hat on a separate bill.

"Now get out."

"Absolutely. That's what I am doing." I sat down and put my feet up on his desk. "Now about that money…"

"Get out of my giant house!"

He picked up a tea cup the size of a badger and hurled it at me. I hurried out of the room, knocking over the world's largest maid as I went.

I spent the rest of the day scouring Central City for Blinky. I must have gone over every square inch of the town, but he just wasn't anywhere. I couldn't understand that. People don't just disappear into thin air, unless they're magicians. And even magicians haven't really disappeared. They're hiding in the hat with that rabbit. I was sure Blinky must be hiding somewhere too, but darned if I could find him. Then, just as I was about to give up, I found him.

I was passing by an art museum and happened to glance in the window. Hanging on one of the walls among the Old Masters was a painting titled: "Frank Burly". It was a portrait of Blinky. He was wearing my hat and smirking.

I ran inside, grabbed the painting, and started shaking it like a rat, saying things like "Now I gotcha!" and "Get that paint off your face and come out of there!"

Security people instantly hurried over and restrained me—using more force than they strictly had to, if you ask me. Trying to drown me in that sink wasn't necessary—then they removed the painting from my grasp and hung it back on the wall, giving me a dirty look as they did so. It was forbidden to damage the museum's paintings, they said, except on special days.

I asked about the painting—who painted it, and how could I get in touch with the model? They said it was a Rembrandt, painted in 1643. I said I didn't understand. They told me to take an art course. I said I might.

After I had glanced at the painting one more time, and then taken it off the wall again and shaken it vigorously, hoping Blinky might fall out of it somehow, the security people grabbed me again. They showed me the door, then threw me through it.

I said: "I've been thrown out of better art museums than this."

"There aren't any better art museums than this."

"Then I take back what I said."

CHAPTER THREE

I didn't understand how there could be a centuries-old painting of a guy I had just got through chasing down the street—that didn't make chronological sense to me. I like things to happen in order. In fact, I insist on it—but the fact that I didn't understand it didn't really bother me too much. There are a lot of things I don't understand. Over five thousand of them now. What's one more? What bothered me was that Blinky was using my name in that centuries-old painting. Now the art connoisseurs would be getting us mixed up! This had to stop.

I went back to the exact spot where I had lost Blinky and looked around. Maybe I could get a handle on where he went if I started from there.

I spent over an hour checking out the whole area, but I couldn't find anything that would help me. No footprints leading away to hiding places full of Blinkys. No tell-tale trail of bread crumbs with a Blinky at the end. Nothing.

I was just turning away to leave when I noticed

a slight distortion in the air in the shape of a hole at the point where Blinky had disappeared. It was so faint you couldn't see it if you were looking directly at it. You had to kind of catch it out of the corner of your eye.

I put my hand in the middle of this distortion and not only did my hand vanish, but I could feel it being sucked down deeper into the hole. I yanked it out, after some effort. Then I put an eye to the hole. Same thing happened. What was going on here?

I looked around, found a cat, and experimentally tossed it in. The cat disappeared, and moments later an ancient statue of the cat approving an important law appeared on the street nearby.

I called over a nearby policeman and pointed out the hole to him. He looked at where I was pointing and then said that I was imagining things.

"Yes," I said, pointing again. "I'm imagining that hole right there."

"I see no hole."

I noticed the cop seemed a little nervous. He was putting his finger in his collar to let the steam out of his neck. I got the feeling he was hiding something.

"You're not hiding something are you? Because I hate that."

"No, of course I'm not," he said, steam belching out of his uniform.

"Okay, then."

"And neither is anyone else."

"Good."

"Now, if you'll excuse me, I have to go be a policeman."

He started to walk away.

"I notice you're walking around the hole," I said.

"I wouldn't know because I can't see it."

After he left I played around a little more with the hole, tossing stuff into it and listening to hear if it hit the bottom. But nothing I threw seemed to hit anything, and my ears kept getting sucked into the hole, so I finally decided to call it a day. I'd throw everything else into the hole tomorrow.

I thought about everything I had seen that day over some coffee and crullers at the donut shop. None of it made much sense to me. I didn't know what this hole thing I had discovered was, or if it had any connection to Blinky's disappearance. I didn't know why that policeman was acting so screwy. I didn't know anything. That was disappointing to me. You'd think I'd know something by now.

The crullers were another disappointment. It's not that they weren't good, they were, but I had to pay full price for them. The donut lady, Mrs. Donatelli, didn't have any day-old donuts today. I was unhappy about this. Day-old donuts aren't as good as new donuts—the Donuts Of Today— but they're a lot cheaper. You can get more for your donut-eating dollar. Day-old irregularly shaped donuts that have fallen behind the cash register and gotten chewed around the edges by something that lives back there are even cheaper. I could write a book about donut prices. And a movie based on that book. That's how well I know donut prices. But on this particular day there weren't any day-old donuts left, and I had to pay full price. You might think that I'm going on over-long about this donut business, but I'm not. This is important. I like donuts. Besides, it's part of the plot.

I asked the donut lady why she didn't have any day-old donuts today, and she started acting all evasive and nervous, and didn't seem to want to talk about it. This surprised me because day-old donuts were always one of her pet peeves. She had always griped about having to sell day-old donuts for less. They didn't cost her any less to make. It was strange she didn't want to talk about it now. But not strange enough to be interesting to me. I changed the subject.

"Are those new tongs?" I asked, as she fished a donut out of the grease.

She dropped the tongs and looked at me like I was a bomb that had just gone off. "No!" she said. "Why do you ask? What in God's name are you implying?"

I shrugged. "I dunno." I didn't want to get into a big fight about it. I was just making conversation. I changed the subject again. "Where'd you get the solid gold hat?"

She looked stricken. Her eyes darted away. I moved my chair so we would still be looking at each other, but her eyes darted away again. I moved my chair one more time—this time for sure, I figured—but as soon as I got settled her eyes started darting all over the place. I quit moving my chair. Losing battle. Finally she answered me: "Um... my rich aunt died..." she said, nervously, "and... it rolled off her head."

"Oh, I see."

I didn't pursue the subject. One of the things I've noticed about life is that the best way to hide something is to act so crazy when people bring it up that they drop the subject immediately and never mention it again. It works every time. It's not that you're fooling anybody—they know you're hiding something—but they're never going to find out what it is. Not if they have to get the information from you. It's not worth it.

As I walked home from the donut shop, I added the donut lady going ballistic for no reason to the list of unusual things that I had seen that day. Something strange was going on. Right here in Central City. But it got stranger the next day. That's when I found the million year old Everly Brothers tape embedded in the cliff face.

I tried to get the tape out—it was one I didn't have, and this was a chance for me to get a free copy made of rock—but I just ended up breaking it. It probably wouldn't have played in my machine anyway. Near the tape was a fossilized Hula Hoop, a copy of last week's newspaper embedded in four million year old amber, and a fossilized stool pigeon who I could have sworn I had gotten some information from just the day before. And yet there he was, embedded in granite, with his arm around a dinosaur.

I was even more surprised when I discovered that no one in town was interested in the strange things I had found. The cops weren't interested in the fossils I showed them, even though one of the fossils appeared to be the jawbone of their police chief. Neither were the newspapers, TV reporters, scientific organizations, or any of our town's crackerjack environmental groups. I would have thought that they all would have been very interested in my discoveries, but about the only reaction I ever got was a nervous cough.

I did get a big reaction from one company I talked to about some automotive products of theirs I had found in an archeological dig, stuffed into the head of a mummified Boy King. All through our conversation they were talking way too loud and sweating way too much.

"Hey, do you have to talk so loud?" I said to the company vice president. "You're hurting my ears. And I'm slipping in your sweat. If you wouldn't mind a little friendly advice, if you're going to lie to your customers, try being a little more cool about it."

"Don't tell us how to run our business," he said, getting louder and sweatier by the second. "I'll have you know our company has been lying to its customers since 1923."

"And sweating?"

"Yes, and sweating. Sweating plenty. And it

hasn't hurt our business any. Stay out of things you don't understand."

"That's good advice, I guess," I admitted.

"It's damn good advice."

"Well, don't swear."

After a few more days of everybody brushing me and my science-shattering chronology-busting archeological discoveries aside like they didn't matter, I started to get annoyed. It wasn't just that everybody seemed to be hiding something, it was that they all seemed to be specifically hiding it from me. I wanted to know what was going on too. Don't forget me. Don't forget about old Frank. He wants in on it too, whatever it is. But no one would tell me anything.

I decided I would have to use more direct methods if I was ever going to find out what was going on. Asking people nicely wasn't working as well as it usually does. So, over the next few nights I stealthily broke into businesses, environmental organizations, even the police station, rifling through their papers, flashing my flashlight on everything, opening safes, just generally poking around looking for clues.

Not only did I not come up with anything—didn't even know what I was looking for really—most of the time I got caught red-handed breaking into these places and found myself with a lot of explaining to do. I tried that talking loud and sweating idea that I got from that company vice president, but it didn't work for me. I guess lying your ass off is harder than it looks.

I got hauled away by the police so many times they started to think I was crazy. I encouraged this idea by playing the harmless eccentric.

"Up is down," I told the policemen when they caught me.

"What?"

"In is out."

They didn't know why I was saying these things, and I wouldn't tell them, but I'll tell you, as long as you promise not to repeat it to them. I was trying to appear crazy so I would be "innocent by reason of insanity". I've got this whole legal system of ours figured out. If you're crazy the law doesn't want you hanging around their jail gibbering and making your eyes go around in circles, and driving everybody else crazy too. They want you out roaming the streets where you belong. So no matter what you've done, all you have to do is talk crazy and there's a good chance you'll walk. And if it doesn't end up working there's always a chance that making nonsensical statements will short circuit the policemen's literal police minds. Then you can escape while they are all in a trance.

"Five is six," I said.

"He's crazy," said a policeman. "Let him go."

"I would think being crazy would be an additional reason not to let him go," said a rookie cop.

"In is out," I said.

"Get him out of here," insisted the first

policeman. "He's not only crazy, he's starting to repeat himself."

They'd argue about it for awhile, but they always ended up letting me go in the end. Each time they did, I'd run out and start breaking into the next building down the street, usually with the same results.

Finally I gave it up. It was no use. There was something going on, that much was obvious, but whatever it was, it would have to go on without me. I was finished with it.

On my way home I stopped in at the donut shop, which is where I usually go when I have given up on something important. It was closed at that time of night, of course—everything is, it's too dark—but by that point I wouldn't have known how to get into a place that was open. I was too used to breaking in to places.

I broke in, sat down at the counter, found some old coffee in a pot that was standing upright in the sink, a handful of perfectly good donut crumbs, and a napkin that still had a lot of use left in it, on one side anyway, and started eating. What a day, I thought. What a year. What a life.

Suddenly I noticed that there was a low grumbling sound coming from somewhere in the back of the shop. I got up to investigate. Nothing should have been on at that time of night. I was worried there might be another prowler in the donut shop besides me.

In the back I found a monstrous machine humming away, busily doing something. It didn't look like it was making donuts, at least no donuts were coming out of it anywhere that I could see, but it was definitely doing something. Maybe the donuts were coming out of the back, I thought. I checked out this theory. Nope. Nothing coming out of the back.

Then I figured that maybe there was a storage area inside the machine where the freshly made donuts were stored and kept piping hot. And maybe there was a place in there where I could sit down and eat those donuts. With a lamp so I could read something while I was eating. This place was starting to sound pretty great to me. Why hadn't somebody told me about this place before? I tried to jimmy the machine open, figuring I could pay for whatever donuts I ate the next time I came back—though, of course, if I ate enough donuts now, I'd never have to come back—but it was no go. There was just no way to get the machine open. I looked over the controls and flipped a few of the switches on and off. I found I could make the machine make more racket, or less, but not donuts. I flipped the switches a couple thousand more times. Same thing. Nothing. Finally I gave it up. I went back to finish my coffee, cursing all machinery, and the wise-guys who built machines that didn't do anything except make a humming noise. I mean, what's the point of making a machine like that? I'm not a violent man, but right then I felt like slapping their face.

On my way home, a couple of people walking in front of me suddenly vanished. I thought that was pretty odd. But odd things had been happening all week. I was too tired to look into it. Screw it. I'm just going home.

CHAPTER FOUR

On my way to work the next morning, I noticed the city seemed a lot less crowded than normal. I was pleased by that. More sidewalk for me. More parking places, too. It looked like the Administration's plan to reduce congestion in the city by making stupid laws and being fantastic assholes was working.

The crowds were so thin a pickpocket had to go way out of his way to bump into me, then he had a tough time blending back in to the crowd because it was so sparse. I watched him work at it for about fifteen minutes, chuckling to myself, then stifling a guffaw, then roaring with laughter, before he finally managed to blend in enough to get away with my money. I guess I should have stopped laughing for a minute and grabbed him while I had a chance, but I didn't think of it at the time. Didn't think of it until now, as a matter of fact. Oh well, live and learn, that's what I always do.

Despite the good start—I liked the extra elbow

room and the funny pickpockets—the day turned out to be a bust, at least from a business point of view. No clients all day. Not a one. I kept looking out of the window to see if anybody was coming my way, maybe with a troubled look on their face and money in their fists, but I never saw anybody like that. And each time I looked out the window there seemed to be less people out there.

My secretary didn't show up either. She didn't even call or send one of her phony telegrams from the maternity hospital. I get about 80 of them a year. Nobody has that many kids. Who is she trying to fool? Because she's not fooling me. Not anymore. I stopped being fooled after the birth of Little Joey #74.

There wasn't any mail delivery today either, even though it wasn't a weekend or holiday. And the morning paper hadn't come, even though it was the morning. What a nothing day.

There was a fly in the office, so I had a little fun with him, trying to smash him. But then I smashed him. So I looked out the window some more. Now I wasn't just looking for clients, I was looking for flies too.

After awhile I noticed it was getting close to lunchtime so I went downstairs to the coffee shop. The place was empty so I grabbed the best table, the one near the door to the kitchen. I always like to sit there, if it's available, because you get your food a little quicker. The waiter doesn't have to walk so far with it.

After an hour had gone by and no one had

taken my order yet, I took a closer look around the place. Not only were there no other customers, there weren't any waiters either. And no cashier. I went back to where they made the food. Nobody was back there either. I found a box of crackers and ate that. Not much of a lunch, but it was filling. And it was cheap, since nobody saw me do it.

Since it was such a slow day I decided not to hurry back to the office. A guy who works as hard as I do deserves an afternoon off now and then. But I didn't end up enjoying myself as much as I deserved to. The boxing match I went to was boring—only one boxer showed up. He hit himself for awhile, but the crowd just booed that. So he started hitting the crowd. That really started them booing. That's when I left. And the ball game I went to was a farce. Both teams were undermanned and didn't have a catcher, so the umpire kept getting hit with every pitch. By the fourth inning he was making bizarre decisions, like calling every pitch a home run, and every fart a triple play. It made for an interesting day at the ball park, but it wasn't baseball in the traditional sense.

I went back to my office and took a look out of the window again to see if maybe a client was coming to see me now. And, though I didn't realize it at the time, I was just in time to watch the last person in Central City walk along the sidewalk and suddenly disappear.

I watched a little longer, but I didn't see

anybody else walking on the sidewalk. I craned my neck. Nobody was coming around the corner to get onto my sidewalk either. I began to sense something was wrong. Where were all the people? And where did that last guy go? There was something vaguely familiar about the way he had vanished. I felt I had seen something like that before, in an earlier chapter of my life. I went outside to investigate.

When I got to the exact spot where the man had disappeared I found one of those shimmery holes there, like the one I had seen Blinky disappear into.

I stuck my head into the hole to get a good look, and to ask if there was anybody down there, and if there was, did they need an unlicensed private detective. Nobody answered me. When I tried to get my head out, it didn't want to come. The suction had gotten it and was slowly pulling it in farther. It took awhile, but after a lot of yanking and cursing and muttered threats about what I was going to do if this head didn't come out pretty damn quick, I finally managed to get it out.

I checked myself over to make sure I was okay and discovered that I wasn't. My hair had all been sucked off, and my face was stretched so badly it was hanging down on my chest. I was horrified for a second, but when I saw my reflection in a store window I had to laugh. I had to admit I was pretty funny looking. "Why the long face?" I asked myself, chuckling. You've got to have a sense of humor about these things. You have to laugh through your tears. It doesn't make any sense, but that's what you're supposed to do. Everybody says so. Still, I was glad when my face gradually worked its way back to its normal position on the front of my head. I mean, it was funny, but it wasn't that funny.

Then it occurred to me that if there were two of these shimmery holes, maybe there were three. There might even be four. (But no more than that.) I squinted and kind of looked sideways at everything out of the corner of my eye, which is how you spot these things, and suddenly saw about three thousand of them. There were holes everywhere. It was only by chance, apparently, that I hadn't walked into one of them on the way here. I decided I'd better watch where I was walking from now on. You're never too old to learn. (William Shakespeare, Page 5.)

I looked for somebody to tell about this, maybe they could fix it, maybe for free, but I couldn't see anyone anywhere. No people, no traffic, there weren't even any lights on in any of the buildings. It looked like I was the only person in Central City left.

For the next few hours I checked out the city from one end to the other, picking my way carefully between the holes, looking into empty buildings, banging on doors, peering under parked cars, yelling "Fire!" into theaters (no law against that), and so on. But I didn't find any signs of life at all. At one point I heard a telegraph transmission sending out some kind of random message, but when I tracked it down it turned out to be coming from an empty theater that was playing the movie: "On The Beach".

For awhile I thought I heard somebody a long ways away from me, who kept repeating everything I said, in my voice. I looked for him for about an hour, with a lot of "Where are you?" and "Where are you?" back and forth. At one point I felt we were pretty close to each other, so I started running excitedly towards him. He started running too, then stopped when I did. And when he burped, so did I. It was uncanny. Finally I stopped looking for him. Even if there was another guy out there, he sounded boring. Get some original material, why don't you, whoever you are. That's what I told him. When he said the same thing back to me, I said I give up. He said he gave up too.

I went all the way out to the city limits looking for signs of life, but found nothing. Even more ominous, I saw there were holes stretching away from Central City as far as I could see, all the way to the horizon. I wondered how far they went. And what they were for. And what, if anything, they were worth—maybe I could make some money out of this. Then I realized that the TV would know. The TV knows everything.

I hurried home and turned on the TV. I figured the newsmen would be having a field day with this story. They probably already had special reports put together; "Empty City: Day 1!" or

"Central City: The 'Hole' Story"—something catchy like that. Make up your own great title, if you don't like the ones I've suggested. Whatever the title, this was going to be good, I knew that.

To my disappointment, there wasn't anything on TV about the people disappearing, or the mysterious holes. In fact, there wasn't anything on TV at all. Just static on every channel. I called a couple of TV repairmen, but they didn't answer their phone. So I tried to fix the television myself. That's how I got this big burn mark on the back of my head. See there? It doesn't hurt anymore, but the mark is still there. Anyway, that's how I got it.

I tried the radio, but got nothing but static on that too. Same thing with the internet. And my cat. I didn't like the way this was looking. It was beginning to appear that this might not be just a local story.

I decided to call the President of the United States in Washington, D.C. about this. I hated to bother him—he was probably busy leading our nation somewhere, to a bold new future maybe—but this was an emergency. The call went through, but all I got was an answering machine. I left a message to "Call Frank", then phoned the leader of Russia. This was no time for partisan politics. I was willing to forget our differences until this crisis was over, if the Russians were. But nobody was home in Russia either. "Call Frank" I told their answering machine, then I started dialing China's number.

14,612 phone calls later the truth began to dawn on me. Everybody on Earth was gone. The planet was empty.

Apparently I was The Last Detective Alive.

CHAPTER FIVE

At first I didn't like the idea of being the last person on Earth. The last detective, sure, I liked the sound of that. That's a hell of a claim to make. In fact, I printed up some business cards that said that. Thousands of them. And I put "The Last Detective Alive" on the back of my suit. But I didn't want to be the last person period. That wouldn't be good for business. I mean, how was I going to make a living now? Who would hire me if I was the only guy here? Figure it out for yourself. It doesn't work, does it? Not to get too philosophical about it, but without life, who pays Frank? Nobody, that's who. And who would be around to read my suit? Nobody again. But it didn't take me long—less than two days—to realize that I didn't need to make a living anymore. The whole world, and everything in it, was mine. I was rich.

A few days later my house was completely full of money, liquor, expensive furniture, fancy clothes, big screen TVs, everything. Heh heh, I thought, looking over my treasure trove, heh heh heh heh heh.

It was only after I had gotten everything into my house, and figured out how to hook up all the electronic stuff (more or less), and managed to get the closet doors to close and stay closed, that I realized I could have just moved to a better house—one that had a lot more room, and already had most of this stuff in it. There was a house just like that right down the street. I had been lugging heavy furniture past it all day. For a second I considered moving, but it had been too much work getting everything here. I didn't want to do it all over again. Screw it. I would just stay here. Kind of too bad, though. I used to like my house full of treasures. Now it just made me mad.

For the first week I checked my mailbox regularly. Maybe all the people who had left would remember to write and tell me when they were coming back. Or how to get to where they were. But after awhile I realized there weren't any mailmen to deliver the letters, even if somebody did send me one. I stopped checking the mailbox after that. No point.

I still got phone calls, plenty of them. But they were all just those automated sales calls. Since I was the only guy left in the world, they kept calling me. The automated voices started to sound pretty desperate after awhile. Finally I unplugged the phone when the calls started getting abusive. I don't have to take that.

Despite the lack of human companionship, or maybe because of it, I really enjoyed myself over the next few weeks. Finally I didn't have to buck the crowds everywhere I went. There were no lines at the theaters. I got great seats at the ball park, right on the pitcher's mound. At nightclubs I had the whole dance floor to myself. At the carnival every turn was my turn. And I finally won the Central City Talent Contest.

You'd think I'd get tired of it after awhile—not being able to share my good life with others—but I never did. It's not the sort of thing a sane person would get tired of.

I also enjoyed the kind of freedom that's unheard of these days in even the freest society. If I wanted to drive the wrong way down the street at an unsafe speed, I could do so. And if I wanted to drive safely, I could do that as well. Society's rules no longer applied to me. There was nothing I couldn't do, no place I couldn't go, no window I couldn't break, and no word I couldn't say on television. It was paradise.

I also was free of the conventions of having to wash, or comb my hair, or make sure my tie was on straight all the time. It didn't matter what I looked like, because no one was there to see me. After a couple of weeks of being free of society's conventions, of being a free spirit, I caught a look at myself in the mirror. I was a mess. It was unbelievable. Where did all the mud come from? And how did that carton of eggs get on my head? I cleaned myself up a little better after that. Go ahead and call me a square if you want. At least I'm a clean square, with a clean straight tie.

Eventually I started to realize that there is a downside to being alone in the world. No, wait, hear me out. There is. If everybody's gone, see, there's nobody around to make anything. So after awhile you start running out of the things you need. My food supplies, for example, were getting dangerously low. I'd always had the vague idea that food grew in supermarkets, with the price stickers already attached by nature. Apparently there's more to it than that. People are involved in food production in some way we don't understand. And Central City was fresh out of people at the moment. As a result, the existing supply of food was disappearing fast. I'd already eaten most of the food in the supermarkets. And a lot of what was left was rotting faster than I could eat it, forcing me to eat more and more rotting food to get the same rotten nutrition.

I was also running out of gasoline, liquor, and dynamite, and there weren't any more clean toilets in town. Something had to be done. But there wasn't anybody around to do it. That's when I started to miss the society of others. That's when I started to learn my lesson.

I say I was alone, but I wasn't really. There were a lot of animals around. Around my house, in fact. They were looking in my windows and hurling themselves against my door. They had noticed the growing lack of food too. And they had also noticed that I had most of what was left.

So they gathered around my place, demanding to be fed. I fed them, but paradoxically that just attracted more animals! Explain that, if you can. And if I didn't feed them, they got unpleasant about it.

"Bring out the food and nobody will get hurt," demanded their spokesman, a parrot.

"Who taught you to say that?" I yelled.

"Squawk."

I gave them as much food as I could spare, but they never seemed to think it was enough. I tried to explain to them that times were tough and we were all going to have to cut back until things got better, until our ship came in, but they weren't buying it. The parrot said I was going to have to come up with a better story than that. I asked him how much time I had to think of a better story and he said twenty four hours.

Around this time is when I first started noticing dusty bills, tickets, fines, and subpoenas appearing on my desk each morning. They were all fantastically old, and none of them made any sense to me. One said I owed 3 Pine Tree Shillings for renting the Mayflower. And apparently the Last of the Mohicans was suing me for calling him an asshole. I brushed these bills aside, after glancing over them. Just a mistake, I thought. Still, it was nice to get some mail again. Even old, misdirected, bullshit, mail.

Then, during one of my walks through town— accompanied by a pack of increasingly wild animals who were following closely behind me, eyeing me, kind of waiting for me to make a mistake, which is, I guess, what animals always do. I just hadn't noticed it until now—I came across a large statue in the park I'd never seen before, of somebody I'd never heard of in my life. I was pretty sure the statue hadn't been there yesterday. But I've never really trusted my memory—at least I think I haven't—so I decided to go to the library to see if I could find out when the statue had been put up, and who the big fat guy on the horse was.

It took me awhile to find the library. I've never been much of a guy for reading. I've always figured I knew too much already. Why make myself more of an egghead than I already am? But I finally located it. It was right across the street from my house. That explained all the "Shh!" noises I'd heard coming from that building over the years.

The library had plenty of history books to choose from, so I picked out the one that had the most pictures and the fewest words and started thumbing through it. I was just looking for information about the statue, but I found a lot more. It looked like all of history had gone screwy. The picture of Napoleon on page four, for example, showed him wearing a sombrero and a basketball uniform. That didn't seem right to me. That wasn't his usual outfit, as I remembered it. And he had his hand in his mouth instead of his shirt. That seemed wrong too. And Davy Crockett was wearing a raccoon coat instead of a raccoon hat.

And everybody at Custer's Last Stand was sitting down.

But the most surprising thing I kept seeing in this book was my own name. It was everywhere. The name "Frank Burly" was like a rash throughout history. Who knocked over the cow that started the Chicago Fire? Frank Burly! Who was the first one to be depressed in the Great Depression? Frank Burly! Who finished off the dinosaurs and then went after the elephants? Frank Burly! Who shot Jesse James six times before Bob Ford even got there? Frank Burly!

Reading all this amused me at first. Just a coincidence, I thought. And there's nothing that amuses me more than a coincidence. It was probably some other Frank Burly they were talking about. Maybe my dad.

But then I came across a picture of "Frank Burly" on an Old West wanted poster. It was Blinky! I stared at it—first in amazement, then in anger. So that was it! Blinky had gone back in time somehow and was running around posing as me, and giving me a bad name in the history books!

The more I thought about this, the madder I got. I don't mind having a bad name now. I've kind of earned it. But not throughout history. Children read history books. School children.

I stormed out of the library and ran to the hole Blinky had disappeared into, which I now realized was some kind of time portal, and started firing my gun into the hole. Then I threw the empty gun into it. Then I started yelling into the hole and shaking my fist—yelling with such force and conviction that I fell into the hole and disappeared into time.

CHAPTER SIX

I guess I've fallen into more holes than anyone in my generation. Look into any hole, I've always said, and there's a pretty good chance I'm there. I've always blamed society for this—they dug the holes. They should have known what was going to happen—but, to be fair, it's probably mostly my own fault. I don't know why I always start losing my balance and waving my arms around in circles and saying: "Ope ope ope!" every time I get near a hole, but I do. Anyway, the point is it's pretty hard to surprise me when it comes to holes. I've had too much experience with them. But this was the first hole I'd ever fallen into that was coated on the inside with powdered sugar.

I was falling down what seemed to be a white translucent tube. Every time I bounced off the sides I got powdered sugar on me. There was some sticky raspberry stuff on the walls too—the stuff they squirt into donuts. Not to be clever, stop me if I'm being clever, for God's sake don't let me start being clever in any way whatever you do, but I felt like I had been swallowed by a policeman.

Just after I had discovered that the powdered sugar on the walls tasted pretty good, and the raspberry wasn't bad either, and hey, what's this pink stuff over here, I bounced extra hard off of one of the walls, veered off at an angle through an opening in the side of the tube, flew end over end through the air and landed on my back in a field.

I got to my feet and looked around. I had no idea where, or when, I was, but I saw there was a cluster of buildings off in the distance, so I started heading that way.

It turned out to be a fairly large town, made up of rudimentary gray buildings built along narrow unpaved and unmarked streets. The people walking these streets were stern looking individuals, with buckles on their hats and superior smirks on their pocked faces. If I'd had to guess where I was, I would have said Las Vegas, but I would have been wrong. It turned out to be Puritan New England—Boston 1680, to be exact.

I figured Blinky had to be around here somewhere. We both had gone down the same hole. So he should have come out where I did, right? Right. Maybe that guy over there was him. Or the little squirt next to him. I started running up to people, spinning them around and saying: "Now I've got you, you little prick". Then I'd have to apologize, saying things like: "Sorry, Reverend",

"Beg your pardon, ma'am", or "Excuse me, Your Majesty".

I showed everybody I met a picture I had brought along of Blinky, explaining that I was looking for this man, and the sooner I found him the sooner I would stop spinning them around and calling them pricks, but they weren't of any help. They hadn't seen anybody that small and flat before and were frightened by it. Even after I had explained what a picture was they still kept running away from it, yelling: "A p-p-picture!"

I found the people of 1680 to be very difficult to deal with. They were all ridiculously arrogant, for one thing. They had names like "Purity", "Patience", "Diligence", and "Humility", and worked hard to live up to their prefabricated reputations. All they wanted to do was brag about their humility, or frantically try to impress me with their patience. I asked if I could talk to "Intelligence", but they said they'd never heard of him. They didn't think he lived around here.

Everyone I met seemed to be fantastically simple, superstitious, posturing, vain, and stupid. And yet modern Americans are descended from these preposterous simpletons! You explain it. I can't.

The most obnoxious of the bunch was a fat guy I ran into on the street named Cotton Mather. He watched me frightening passersby with my picture of Blinky for awhile then waddled up to me and said: "Begone, witch!"

"You begone, asshole," I replied. I don't begone

just because someone tells me to. I begone when I want to.

He stepped back a pace in surprise, then advanced again and shook a pudgy finger in my face. "Necromancer!" he said.

"Asshole!"

"Demon!" he shouted.

"Asshole!"

At this point he noticed that a crowd had begun to gather to watch this shouting match, and sensed the indignity of his position. I think he was also beginning to run out of insults, while I wasn't even close to running out. "I will deal with thee later, witch!" he said as he made a hasty exit, putting his hands over his ears so he couldn't hear my reply, which, just for the record, was "asshole".

As I resumed my search for Blinky, I kept noticing huge piles of junk on the street. Not Colonial junk, but junk from my era. There were stacks of 8-track tapes, Polavision players, 2009 calendars, and all kinds of other crap. The locals were looking at these piles worriedly, and making wide circles around them when they went by.

After I'd gone around several of them myself, I started to get tired of it.

"Hey, aren't you people going to clean this up?" I asked.

They shook their heads.

"We're afraid of it," explained one of the men.

"The Devil put it there," said another man.

"Oh," I said.

I started walking around the pile.

"Will you clean it up?" a third man asked, hopefully.

"Hell, no. Not if the Devil put it there." I'm not stupid. I don't need that kind of trouble.

I did look through the pile a little bit. I figured the Devil wouldn't mind that. If I found something I liked maybe I could trade him something for it. Something I would never miss. But there was nothing I wanted. All the electronics were out of date. The magazines were back numbers. The fashionable clothes were more out of fashion than mine were. It was just junk.

On top of one of the piles I passed there was an old tube television which had somehow gotten going and was showing a Beta videotape of an episode of Bewitched. The flickering images plainly frightened the people, but nonetheless they seemed strangely drawn to them. Old women with warts on their noses were watching the show with particular fascination, occasionally trying to twitch their noses like the little witch in the box was doing. But they usually couldn't do it and had to resort to using their hands to manually twitch their noses. Or rub their noses back and forth against something hard—like a fence.

The common people didn't understand everything they were seeing in these flickering images, but fortunately church leaders were there to explain: there were two Darrins because the first one had been sent to Hell for marrying a witch. And the show went downhill after the third season because it got new writers—the old writers being sent to Hell for writing about witches. I was about to laugh at this childish explanation, but then realized it was probably right. It was the only thing that made sense, now that I thought about it.

Searching for people is thirsty work, so I was grateful when I happened on a tavern. I went inside, and the first thing I noticed was that there was a guy from my era there. He was easy to spot, because he was the only person in the place who wasn't scared to death. Everyone else was backed into a corner and staring at him with wide eyes, with a few thumbing through their Bibles to see what could be done about him.

I sat down at his table and introduced myself. He said his name was Harrison. I showed him my picture of Blinky. He said he hadn't seen him. I ordered a drink, then pointed out to Harrison that he and I seemed to be back in time, and he said yes, he'd noticed that too. I asked him how we had gone back in time in Central City and ended up in Boston. I didn't get that part of it. I understood the time travel, but not the road trip.

"Time is like a river," he explained.

"Is it?"

"Exactly like a river." He took a drink, then added: "It washes people from place to place. And so forth."

"That's not a very thorough explanation," I said, critically.

"Hey, I'm an appliance salesman. What do you expect?"

"Oh. Sorry. I thought you were some kind of time travel expert."

"No, I'm the Midwest sales representative for the Novelty Appliance Corporation of America, manufacturers of the Original Talking Vacuum Cleaner. 'It Talks As It Cleans'."

"What does it talk about?"

He shrugged. "It mostly just complains about all the work it has to do. Want to buy one?"

"No."

His face fell, but he didn't pursue the matter. He put away the brochure he'd been showing me, and took his arm from around my shoulders.

My drink arrived and was spilled in my lap by a frightened waitress. She asked if I wanted another one. I said not right now, I was still wet from the first one.

I asked Harrison if everybody from Central City had ended up here in Boston like we did. I was hoping this was so, because I didn't want to have to go to a lot of different places to find Blinky. I wanted to find him right here. Sitting at the table with us, if possible. Or fast asleep in my outstretched arms. Harrison said he didn't think that was the way it worked. He'd only seen a few people from the 21st Century here. He figured we were probably spread out all over history, time being like a river like it is. I asked what made him think time was like a river, and he said don't let's start that again.

"Your man could be anywhere," he said. "There's no way to control where you come out of the time tube, so if he isn't here, there's no way of knowing where he is."

I thought about this, then said I guessed I might as well go back home then. Back to good old 2010. The thought cheered me up. It would be nice to get back where I belonged. It's true that the food was running low up there, but if worst came to worst I could always eat that parrot. That would hold me for awhile. And maybe he knew some other parrots.

Harrison broke in on my thoughts. "You can't go back."

I balled up my fists. "Who's going to stop me? You?"

He shook his head. "Physics."

I stared at him blankly.

"One of the sciences," he explained.

My stare got blanker.

He took out a piece of paper and a pencil to diagram what he was talking about for me. Everyone in the tavern screamed in terror when he pulled out the pencil, then screamed even more when it began making marks on the paper, practically by itself.

"Don't mind them," Harrison said, "they're afraid of everything. Now, here's us in 1680." He drew a line on the paper, then added two little pictures of us partway along the line.

"I like it that you've given me a big smile," I said, smiling along with the picture.

"There are caps on both ends of the time tube, see? You can travel anywhere in the past in the tube, but you can't get out at either end."

"I think I see a way out right there," I said, pointing.

He closed up the line at the end.

"Oh," I said. I was disappointed. There went the only possible way out that I could see.

I glumly ordered another drink and waited for it to be poured in my lap with the others. I was starting to like it.

"A talking vacuum cleaner isn't just a novelty item, you know," Harrison said.

"What else is it?"

"It's an indispensable part of any talking home."

"Ah."

"Think about it."

"I will."

"Talk it over with your toilet."

"Okay."

I paid my bill, wished Harrison luck, waved to the other people in the tavern, which caused two of them to drop dead and one of them to spring apart, and started making my way back to the time tube. I wasn't completely convinced there was no way to get home. Because if I couldn't get home, well, that would be awful. So before I would believe it, I would have to see it for myself.

It turned out there was a bit of a delay before I could find out whether Harrison was right or not, because on the way to the time tube I was arrested and tried for witchcraft.

Apparently, the little fat guy I'd argued with on the street—Mather—had found someone who was willing to swear that I had turned her into a noisy little girl.

When I was brought face to face with my accuser in court she looked like a little girl, all right. She said she used to be the Governor of Connecticut until I came along.

"Jesus!" I said, impressed. "And you say I did this?"

"Yes."

"How?"

She said I'd been having concourse with the Devil, naturally, that's how these things were always done. And that I had enlisted the Evil One's aid to not only turn her into a little girl, but also to make one of the goats in town smell bad. The goat was brought in to back up her story, which it did masterfully.

"Looks like I'm a witch, all right," I said, scratching my head. This was all news to me, but I couldn't deny the facts. There was the little girl. And the Governor of Connecticut was nowhere to be seen. And the goat smelled just as bad as she said it would.

"You admit you are a witch?" asked the judge.

I shrugged. "I guess so."

"Then you may go," he said.

"Huh?"

"You have admitted you are a witch, therefore you cannot be a witch."

"Run that one by me again."

He looked at me like I was a simpleton. "Satan will not allow his servants to admit their allegiance to him. You have admitted it, therefore the Evil One has no control over you. You cannot possibly be a witch. Don't you know anything about the law?"

"I thought I did, until now."

"Conversely, if you had said you weren't a witch, then we would have known that you were up to something."

Everyone in the courtroom nodded in agreement. That was the way it worked all right.

"Well if I'm not a witch, then who made the little girl smell bad?"

"It's the goat who smells bad," corrected the little girl, crossly. "I am under an entirely different spell."

"A witch did it," explained the judge, his patience wearing thin. "A real witch. Not you. Now stop wasting the court's time, Mister... Not-Witch!"

I stepped down from the stand and started to make my way out of the disappointed courtroom.

"Now," said the judge, looking around the room, "who denies being a witch?"

Several hands went up.

"Burn them," said the judge. "Anyone else?"

Another hand hesitantly went up.

"Burn him."

I got back to the time tube without further

incident, climbed in, put my hands on the sides of the tube, and gave a push. I started floating up the tube, slowly at first, then faster and faster, until I finally banged my head on the top, hard enough to dent it—my head I mean.

I clung there for a moment, feeling the top of the time tube with my hands. It felt like a spooky manhole cover. I couldn't find any way to open it, so I banged on it with my fist and yelled, hoping to attract the attention of somebody up there— maybe somebody with an axe, or, even better, a beautiful woman in a skimpy bathing suit with tickets to a Broadway show and an axe. But then I remembered that I had been the last one to leave Central City. There couldn't be anyone else up there now. I heard a dog up there growling at the hole, but that was all.

After awhile the dog left—maybe to get a blowtorch and cut me out. At least I hoped that's where he was going. He probably was. I was pretty sure he had some kind of plan in mind. Dogs are smarter than we think—smarter than they look, anyway. But this one wasn't. He came back after awhile, but it was just to growl at me some more.

I clung to the top of the time tube for awhile, glumly thinking over my situation. It didn't look good. It looked like the novelty appliance makers were right, as usual. I appeared to be trapped— trapped in a billion years of history.

CHAPTER SEVEN

I guess I don't have a lot of imagination. That's what people tell me, anyway. I wouldn't have thought of it myself. But they're probably right. Now that I found myself stranded in the past the only place I could think of to go was back to 1680. Good old 1680. That seemed like home now. I could go to that tavern again. And order that same drink. Maybe get tried as a witch again. I knew how to do that. It wasn't much of a life, but it was all I knew at this point. I started heading back.

It didn't take me long to discover that Harrison had been right about traveling around in time. Once you were in the tube there was no way to know where you were going to come out. You knew which direction you were heading—forward in time or back—but that was all. And there were no markings in the interior of the tube to indicate which year you were passing through, or which exit was which. They should fix that, I thought. If I had a time tube, mine would have year markings. And everybody would like my time tube best.

I'd been traveling back in time all the time I was thinking about this, so I decided I had probably gone far enough now. This was about where 1680 should be, by my reckoning, so I stepped out in caveman days—into the mouth of the first lion.

The lion was as surprised as I was, so when his jaw dropped in astonishment and he made a kind of "What?" sound it gave me a chance to make a graceful, if hasty, exit. Then I took a look around.

Well, I thought 1680 was primitive. This place was even worse. There were no buildings at all. People lived in caves, if they could find them. Or on the ground with a "cave view", if that's all they could get. They dressed in dried leaves and crud, and ate the same stuff they were wearing, sometimes while they were wearing it. As before, my first guess was that I was in Las Vegas—maybe somewhere on the Strip, near the casinos—but I soon discovered I was wrong. This was prehistoric Earth. Not Vegas.

There were huge piles of obsolete 21st century junk all over the landscape, just as there had been in 1680, but the cavemen didn't seem to mind the contamination. They had no fear of it. They were pawing through the rubbish, trying to eat some things, trying to wear others. I saw one caveman pulling out long strands of audio tape and wrapping himself in it until he couldn't move or see, then using the empty tape cartridges as nose-plugs. He looked like a mess to me, but he seemed happy enough. In fact, he seemed to think he looked rather jaunty. Another caveman was wearing some 3-D glasses he had found and seemed alarmed by almost everything he saw, gripping the hand of a nearby caveman whenever he saw something new, though sometimes he seemed delighted by what he saw. Some cavemen found old guns, which, as often as not, they pointed at their own faces. This usually resulted in a lot of primitive laughter when the trigger was pulled.

Seeing the cavemen chewing speculatively on chrome automobile bumpers to see if they tasted any better than the rotary dial telephones and old voting machines they had been eating reminded me that I was hungry, so I inquired about food. It took awhile to get an answer because the cavemen not only didn't speak English, they didn't speak any language of any kind, and weren't planning to. Once I had managed to explain the concept of food to one of the cavemen, using sign language, he explained that we were the food. Everything ate us. Not the other way around. I made the sign language sign for: "What?" And he replied with the sign language for: "You heard me". I decided maybe I should move on to some other time period. I didn't like the food chain around here. It seemed kind of backwards to me.

Before I left, I showed some of the cavemen the picture I had of Blinky. That's when they spoke the first words ever spoken by Man.

"Frank... Burly!" they grunted, angrily.

They pulled out some crap they had evidently been sold and now regretted buying. Then they showed me how empty their primitive wallets were.

"No, no," I said, laughing and pointing to myself. "I'm Frank Burly."

Luckily cavemen are shaped kind of funny and don't run too well. And they're usually so mad they can't see straight. Otherwise they probably would have caught me.

I made it to the time tube just in time and jumped in. The cavemen clustered around the opening waving their shoddy merchandise and demanding a refund, with some of them hopefully holding up their extended warranties, but I was already on my way out of there. They weren't getting any refunds today. Not from this Frank Burly, anyway. And as far as I was concerned, they could shove their extended warranties up their ass.

My experience in prehistoric times made me even madder at Blinky than I had been before. He wasn't just ruining my reputation now, he was putting me in actual physical danger.

This was brought home to me forcibly at my next stop when I just made it back to the time tube one jump ahead of Christ and his 12 Apostles. I don't know what they thought I had done to them, but it must have been something pretty big. I don't think I've ever seen Christ so mad.

Everywhere I went it seemed like my reputation had preceded me. Everybody said I had conned them out of their money, or sold them defective merchandise, or told their daughters things that weren't strictly true. There were warrants out for me in various places for everything from talking total bullshit to murder.

As a result, I kept being run out of town on a rail the minute I arrived and told them who I was. I kept telling them okay, I said I was Frank Burly, and it's true, I am Frank Burly. No, no, wait, let me finish. What I was going to say was: maybe there are two Frank Burlys, did you ever think of that? Or maybe there's twenty two. But they weren't falling for that. Just because they were born yesterday didn't mean they were stupid. They admitted that my face looked a little different than it did before, but they said that was the oldest trick in the book.

And because I had no control over where I traveled in time, I ended up going back to some of the same places again and again. There were times when there were as many as three of me being run out of the same town at the same time on three different rails. Once we even managed to get an impromptu race going. I think I won, but I'm not sure. It's hard to tell me apart sometimes.

I couldn't understand how Blinky had managed to piss off so many different people in so many different places. It didn't seem possible.

The man was a genius. Then I found out he wasn't doing it alone. He had help.

I found this out in 1914 when I ran into a shady looking character who was preparing to assassinate an archduke. He said his name was Frank Burly too. While I helped him pack his bomb with explosives, I asked him where his family came from, because maybe we were related, maybe he was my long lost Uncle Frank. But he said he was just leasing the name to use as an alias from the original Frank Burly—a short guy with a squeaky voice who blinked all the time. This made me mad. I said I was Frank Burly. He said join the club. I said I was already in the club. I was the president of the god damn club. He said he didn't care who the hell I was. We stopped talking after that. I think we both realized we were swearing too much. He went back to work on his bomb, but it was too late now. The archduke had already gone past. Some other Frank Burly down the street got him.

I began running into Frank Burlys wherever I went. There were thousands of them. They were all dressed up to look more or less like me, and carried driver's licenses with my name and their picture on them. They even went so far as to copy my trademark "Burly Walk" (stomach out, one, two, neck back, three, four). It made me mad every time I saw them doing this. They weren't me. I'm me. Stop doing the Burly Walk!

With so many Frank Burlys wandering around I started getting credit for doing more, and bigger, things: gunning down Alexander Hamilton, sinking the fleet at Pearl Harbor, getting the shaking going in the San Francisco Earthquake, starting assorted wars and economic upheavals—you name it, I did it. At least that's what it looked like. I thought I was unpopular before, when I was just being accused of conning ordinary citizens out of a couple of bucks. Now I was making entire governments mad at me. Religions too. A lot of them never had a name for their devil before. Now they did. Sheesh. What a mess.

But as messed up as my life was, history was getting messed up even more. Not only were there those piles of junk from the 21st century screwing things up—the California Gold Rush had to be cancelled. Too many 8-track tapes in the way. Nobody could get past Missouri—now people throughout history were starting to act out of character and dress funny. Everybody at The Last Supper, for example, was wearing an oversized foam rubber cowboy hat. And Spartacus had wristwatches all up and down his arm. There were taxi cabs at the Battle of Gettysburg. And the Know-Nothings knew everything now. Nothing looked right to me. It reminded me of that crazy history book I had been reading back at the Central City library.

I started to wonder if someone was deliberately tampering with the past. And if they were, why? And how would altering the past affect our future? But I didn't wonder about it for long. I had my own problems. Besides, the fact is, I don't really care about things like that—history and mankind's future and so on. Everybody just do what you want, that's my motto. Leave me out of it. If you all end up destroying yourselves, it's all right with me. No skin off my nose. That's the way I look at it. That's my healthy outlook on life.

But pretty soon they started tampering with me too. "They" in this case being a fat guy wearing Bermuda shorts, sunglasses, gold chains around his neck, and a big cigar in his mouth. I ran into him when I was in the Old West.

I had been following what I thought was Blinky's trail, but which turned out to be a rattlesnake's trail. After I got out of the doctor's office, I stopped in at the sheriff's office to look over the wanted posters hanging on the wall. All of them said "Frank Burly", even though the pictures were of different guys. I had just started reading about all the awful things they said I had done—do you know who shot Liberty Valence now? Me! And do you know who Liberty Valance was? Me!—when this guy wearing Bermuda shorts I was telling you about rolled into the office.

"You the Sheriff of Dodge City? Of course you are! You're in the sheriff's office. Who else could you be? Now, from now on I want you to wear tennis shoes and lederhosen, and speak with a Brooklyn accent."

"Who are you?" I asked, looking doubtfully at the lederhosen that had been handed to me by his assistant.

"Youse," the fat man said, correcting me.

"Remember the accent. I'm the guy who's telling 'youse' to wear this lederhosen, that's who I am."

"Yeah, but..."

"You're not questioning my judgment are you? Because the last guy who did that got canned."

"Of course I'm not questioning your judgment, whoever you are, but..."

"Okay, then."

He didn't hang around to argue with me anymore. He had to go put lipstick and brassieres on all the frontier women. Nice work if you can get it. I didn't know who the guy was, but he seemed to be an authority of some kind. And you know what I always say about authorities: We better do what they say. We don't want any trouble from them.

As I was struggling to put on the lederhosen, muttering that they couldn't treat Frank Burly like this, Frank Burly didn't have to put up with this kind of crap, who did they think they were trying to push Frank Burly around like this, and so on, louder and louder, somehow word got out that I was Frank Burly, and I had to abandon my lederhosen and make a run for it. Fortunately I had been run out of so many places by now I was pretty good at it. They hardly caught me at all.

I arrived in Washington, D.C. on April 14th, 1865, with a bullet in my ass and three ropes around my neck. Something about the date stuck in my mind. Then I remembered what it was.

I made my way to Ford's Theater, bought a ticket, and went inside to see the show.

There were a lot of other time travelers there too, I noticed. They knew what was going to happen as well as I did, so everyone in the audience was watching the back of Lincoln's head instead of the play.

I found myself seated next to Charles Darwin, so I chatted with him for awhile while I was waiting for the tragedy to unfold. He said he was working on his next book: The Origin of Baseball. First basemen evolving into second basemen, then third basemen, and so on. I listened politely, then expressed my hope that his theory would someday evolve into a better one. He said that was what he was counting on.

Finally a gunshot went off, Lincoln yelled "Wow!" and slumped forward, and Booth jumped onto the stage and proclaimed: "Sic semper tyrannis! Or my name isn't Frank Burly!" Then he ran off into the wings.

There was a big uproar, of course, with everyone running around yelling: "Did you see what just happened?" and "Somebody call the newspapers!" Then they started looking for the assassin. A few people who were sitting near me looked in my direction.

"Your name is Frank Burly," said one of them.

"Yeah, but that doesn't mean I shot Lincoln," I said, chuckling. "I mean, you saw who did it. It was that guy up on stage there."

They looked at the stage, but Booth was long gone. So they looked back at me.

When I got to the time tube, I tossed aside my

hostage—Lincoln's widow, who had been struggling with me the whole way and yelling that I was driving her insane—and dove into the tube just ahead of half the cops in the 19th century.

I went whizzing off through time, wondering where I would be chased out of next. I hoped it would be Paris. I've always wanted to be chased out of Paris. Ooh la la. Suddenly the tube abruptly ended and I fell out onto the ground.

I got up and looked at the time tube. A huge section of it was gone. All around me medieval guys were chopping up time tubes and stacking up the pieces onto carts. I asked them what they were going to use them for, and they said they didn't know yet. But anything this big had to be good for something. I was starting to suggest that they leave one of the tubes standing, just as a favor to me, (they owed me a favor, I reminded them), when I heard one of the woodsmen say: "Well, that's the last of them", and the last section of time tube in England toppled to the ground.

I looked around. He was right. There weren't any tubes left that I could see. And I could see a long way, because all of the trees had been chopped down too. And they were just finishing stamping the hills flat. I didn't like the look of this. I appeared to be stranded permanently in Medieval England. It looked like I might never see 1680 again.

CHAPTER EIGHT

I made my way to the nearest village, being careful not to tell everyone I met on the way what my name was. I had to be careful about that now, because I didn't have any place to run to anymore now that the time tubes were gone. So, like I said, I hardly told anybody.

Then, just as I was about to start yelling my name from the top of a tower, I hit on the idea of adopting a false name. I guess I should have thought of that sooner. It probably would have saved me a lot of trouble. I will do that next time. I'm writing a note to myself right now.

At first I decided to call myself Blinky. That would teach the bastard. See how he liked having his identity stolen by some jerk. But then I realized this might be confusing to my readers if I ever came to write this all down. Besides, the name didn't really fit me. I don't look like a Blinky. So I decided to call myself Sir Surly the Bold. It was close enough to my real name to make it easy to remember. Plus, it kind of fit my surly personality.

Once I got settled in, I found I liked Medieval England. It was kind of brutal and childish and smelly and stupid, but I managed to fit in there pretty well anyway.

A typical day for us medieval types was usually just spent yelling, misunderstanding things, and getting angry—three things at which I excel. The night time hours were the same except it was darker and colder while you were yelling, which gave you something extra to yell about. Not a great life, I'll grant you, but not bad.

Money for food and lodging wasn't easy to come by in this time period—every coin had to be made by hand, and the government was as lazy as I was, so there wasn't a lot of it around—but I managed to pick up a few bucks here and there. I worked for awhile as a medieval magician. I'm not particularly magical—when I saw a woman in half, I go to jail. And I don't know which card you pulled out of the deck. Give me a hint—but it was pretty easy to astonish people who were this unsophisticated. All I had to do was snap my lighter on and off. When the applause died down, I'd snap my lighter on and off again for an encore. Occasionally I took requests from the audience. They wanted me to snap my lighter on and off. It was an easy job, but boring. And after awhile I got the first recorded instance of carpal tunnel syndrome and the doctors there, after a great deal of consultation, drained the brain out of my head to fix the problem. My thumb did feel a little better after the operation, but I've forgotten my childhood now. Which is too bad because I used to blame all of my problems on that. And now I can't.

I also got a part-time job telling people all was well, when all wasn't well. I was one of those guys. It didn't pay much, but, to be fair, it wasn't much of a service I was providing, either. I was mostly just giving everybody the wrong impression. So I didn't complain too much about the low salary.

It was a pretty good life overall, but, as I said, kind of boring. Until the Spring Festival rolled around, that is. That was the big event they had there every year. If you believed all the pre-festival publicity (and I did), this year's festival was going to be the biggest thing since the sun started revolving around the Earth. It was going to be the medieval equivalent of a blast and a half. Oh boy, oh boy.

I excitedly showed up on the first day of the festival, ready to be entertained like I had never been entertained before, but was quickly disappointed. There was a lot going on all right, but none of it was very interesting. Show business was still in its infancy, is why. There were lackluster competitions (the Shit Kicking Contest, for example), crude entertainments (a pile of shit on a stage), and food that tasted, unless my medieval taste buds deceived me, like shit.

I tried my hand at a few of the games, copping 2nd place in a joust, and had my picture painted standing next to a wooden cut-out of the Antipope.

Then I went over to watch the shit on the stage for awhile. It wasn't too exciting until the second act break, when part of the pile fell over. The audience was stunned. They didn't know what was going to happen next. How was the pile of shit going to get out of this? I didn't hang around to find out. The story didn't have enough plot to hold my interest. And I had a hard time identifying with the main character. So I left early and ended up missing the big climax where, I'm told by someone who was there, the pile of shit suddenly got into a sword fight with some Turks. I wish I'd seen that. That sounds incredible.

I capped off what had turned out to be a very disappointing afternoon by wandering in front of a target and getting shot in the chest by Robin Hood. As I lapsed into unconsciousness the last thing I remembered hearing was that Robin Hood had won.

"He split Sir Surly! The tinker wins! He wins!"

"Wait a minute," said some other archer, "don't I get another shot?"

"The tinker wins the golden arrow!" insisted the primitive public address system at the fairgrounds (a big leather trumpet with a man inside).

Another arrow hit me in the chest, splitting Robin Hood's arrow.

"That shot doesn't count! The tinker still wins! He wins!"

I passed out with more arrows hitting me in the chest as the tournament announcer kept insisting that the contest was over and everybody might as well stop shooting me, because nobody was going to get a prize for it.

I came to in Robin Hood's camp, where I had been brought to be fixed up by a contrite Robin.

"I hope you're not hurt," he said.

"Of course I'm hurt."

"Is your chest okay?"

"Well, it's full of arrow holes, if that's what you mean." I guess that's what he meant.

I asked him if he was the real Robin Hood, because if he was, I had heard of him. Both good things and bad. I had heard, for example, that he robbed from the rich (I smiled), and gave to the poor (I frowned). He said he was the guy I was thinking of, all right, but Robin Hood wasn't his name anymore. His new name, he said, his noble eyes shifting all over the place, was Frank Burly.

Most of his Merry Men were named Frank Burly too, though a couple of them claimed to be Richard the Lionheart, and one guy said he was Jack and the Beanstalk.

"Hiya, Franks," I said, when I was introduced to them. I didn't try to argue with them about it. I didn't care anymore.

"What be your name, stranger?" asked the third Frank Burly from the left.

"I dunno," I said, wearily. "Probably Frank Burly."

"Right," he said, winking broadly.

I asked them how their business was going

these days. They said pretty good. They'd taken a lot from the rich this week—up 9% from last week—but were having trouble finding a poor person to give it to. Once you gave a poor person a lot of money, they explained, he ceased being poor anymore, and this had them worried. It didn't bode well for the future of their organization. Some of Robin's men were already looking around for other work. There was a new Merry Band that had just started up in another forest a few miles up the road, they heard, that set fire to the rich and threw water on the poor. That was close enough to what they were doing now that they thought they might be able to get jobs there.

I joined Robin Hood's band for awhile, and helped them rob and kill and do other good deeds. It was pleasant enough work, but I didn't like sleeping on tree branches. I always woke up about a hundred feet below the branch, with my arms and legs bent all screwy and everybody laughing merrily at me. That was the only downside to the job—those branches. Somebody should cut those branches off.

I learned a lot from my brief association with Robin Hood. For example, he's the one who tipped me off that it's important to get a receipt from the poor when you give money to them. Otherwise you can't deduct it. He said the poor might not want to give you a receipt—they're a suspicious lot—so sometimes you have to lash them.

One of the Merry Men, who was a distant ancestor of Franklin D. Roosevelt, kept arguing that the money should be given to the poor in the form of government employees, but he was shouted down. Too soon, I guess. That idea wouldn't make sense for awhile yet.

It was while this argument was going on that I noticed that one of Robin's Merry Men wasn't taking part. He didn't look particularly Merry either. He looked more Sneaky than Merry. And if he was giving money to any poor people, it was to the poor people who lived in his pocket. I also noticed he kept turning his head away quickly every time I looked at him, and had been doing this ever since I joined up. Finally I went up to him and made his head stay where it was for a minute with my hands so I could see it.

It was Blinky.

"You!" I yelled.

He took off, and I took off after him, howling with triumph. Finally, after all of these millennia, I had found the son of a bitch who... but he had already disappeared again.

"God damn it!" I said.

I stood there cursing a blue streak, while Robin and his men covered their ears. This was very frustrating to me, as you can imagine. It was also very familiar.

I went over and examined the spot where Blinky had disappeared. Sure enough, there was a time tube there. A trick of the light made it harder to see than the others had been. And it was intact.

I dove in, determined to find Blinky again, and this time I wouldn't let him get away for at least an hour. I had some things I wanted to discuss with his rear end.

CHAPTER NINE

This was the beginning of another long futile chase that I'd rather not dwell on. You know how it goes by now: Ha ha! Now I've got you!... hey, where did you go?... Sorry, ma'am... Excuse me, Mr. Hitler. I thought you were some other sneaky little shit... and on and on. Maybe I shouldn't chase people anymore. I'm not good at it. Maybe I'll make that my New Year's resolution.

Not only was the chase futile, it caused a lot of damage too. That's inevitable when you're involved in a headlong chase because you're really not paying attention to the things around you. You're not "looking before you leap", as the kids say. Ever wonder what happened to the dinosaurs? That was my fault. The dinosaurs were doing all right—in fact they were quite a ways along on their Moon Program, I understand. They had their first seven dinosaurs chosen—until Blinky and I ran through the Cretaceous Period without looking where we were going. Now they are extinct. They didn't even last another Period.

So that just shows you what can happen if you don't look where you're going. The Titanic? That was me too. I spotted Blinky on this boat, see, and I said to myself: "I've got to stop that ship! But how?" Well, I guess you know how. You were taught about it in school. So I guess I should apologize for that too. And you know that religion they used to have that worshipped large panes of glass that were so big they had to be carried across the street by two men? That's what happened to that religion. I kind of feel bad about that. But I'm also surprised it lasted as long as it did. Kind of a miracle, really.

Anyway, I suppose you're probably waiting for me to lose Blinky completely again, which I finally did in 1775.

He had jumped out of the time tube, with me right on his heels, as usual. But this time instead of chasing him all over creation for days on end and then coming all the way back to the place where we started, I decided to just wait by the tube for him to circle around and come back. I'm not completely stupid. I've been through this before. I know how it works. I stretched out on the ground, lit up a cigarette, and waited.

A week later all my cigarettes were gone and I found I was getting really cold and hungry. Blinky hadn't come back like he was supposed to—like he had always done before. Something was wrong. I decided not to wait any longer. Reluctantly, I abandoned my post (stuffing a towel in the hole in the tube so no one could get in or out without removing the towel) and started looking for Blinky.

A half hour's walk brought me to the outskirts of a large Colonial town, which turned out to be Philadelphia. It had a lot more contamination from the future than any of the other places I'd visited. Not only were there huge piles of outdated products everywhere, but the air was full of gasoline fumes, smog, powdered sugar, and other 21st century pollutants. There were also a lot of people from my era wandering around town, taking flash pictures of the locals, stripping the town of souvenirs, hitting on all the Colonial women, and just generally making pests of themselves. I don't know why 1775 had so much more contamination than all the other eras. Maybe it was one of those "focal points in time" we hear so much about in the movies. Just because something makes a writer's job easier doesn't mean it's not true. I think 1775 was definitely a "focal point in time".

All the contamination seemed to be really pissing the Colonists off, I noticed. I don't think they liked being a focal point in time. Though, actually, everything seemed to piss off these guys. Everybody in the Colonial Period had a big chip on their shoulder. They argued with each other all the time, about everything.

The biggest source of argument was politics. Everybody knew what was true and what wasn't when it came to politics. What they knew was true, and what you knew wasn't even close. And everybody was armed with facts about the current political situation that nobody else knew but them.

"Tea is made of human beings," I heard one Patriot say.

"And tea," pointed out a Loyalist.

"Well, yes. Human beings and tea. But that's a lethal combination. Benjamin Franklin was saying only this week..."

"Benjamin Franklin is a British spy," said the Loyalist.

"You take that back."

"I'll take it back when he stops being a British spy, and not before."

"Loyal bastard!"

"Patriotic scum!"

That's when the fight started. Nobody else paid much attention to this fight because there were similar fights going on on every street corner. The Colonials certainly seemed to be riled up about something—about everything, as near as I could tell.

There was talk in the Colonies of Revolution—of rising up and killing every Englishman we saw. Others felt we should leave the Englishmen alone. The middle ground, or "common sense position", was to just injure the Englishmen and leave them for dead.

I showed my picture of Blinky around to the people fighting in the streets, but nobody had seen him. Everybody I showed it to asked which side I was on: the right side (pointing at themselves), or the wrong side (pointing at the other guy, who stiffened). I said both sides sounded pretty nutty to me. Which I guess was the wrong answer because I ended up fighting with everybody.

One of the Colonists I showed Blinky's picture to was a grocer named Roderick Snodwell. The name rang a bell. Then I remembered. Mr. Acropolis had an autograph of a guy with that name. From this same era, too. It had to be the same guy. I told Snodwell I knew a guy who had his autograph. He said he'd better give it back, or there was going to be trouble. I said okay, I'd tell him to give it back. He said I'd better, or there would be trouble. I figured I'd better change the subject, so I asked him if that corn was fresh. He said of course it wasn't fresh, get out of his store. Like I said, everybody in those days had a chip on their shoulder.

After Snodwell and I had finished beating each other up, I stopped in at a nearby tavern, which turned out to be a favorite of the Founding Fathers. The place was full of them. I went over to chat with some of them. I figured it would give me something to tell my history teacher about someday.

I walked up to John Hancock.

"John Hancock?" I asked.

He looked at me like I was a creditor, or maybe an angry husband, or a cop. I know that look. In my business you see it all the time. And I use it a lot myself. So does my mom.

"Who wants to know?" he asked, suspiciously.

Now the evasive look appeared on my face. "Uh... I'd rather not say," I said. I didn't know whether the name Frank Burly was mud around here or not, but since Blinky had been here a week already, it probably was.

Hancock sneered at me. "Got something to hide, eh?"

"Maybe."

"Maybe yes, or maybe no?"

"Maybe yes."

He nodded. I could tell he admired the crafty way I was playing this. "Drink?"

"Sure."

After we'd had a few drinks together, and the Founding Fathers had decided I was all right, they told me about the big freedom scam they had going. They'd been working on it for years, they said. The idea, as I understood it, was to get top dollar for the tea they'd been smuggling in from the Dutch East Indies. But they could only get a good price if they could get the British out of the picture. The unscrupulous British, they said, were bringing in cut-rate tea, selling it below cost, and driving the market price down. So nobody was buying the Founding Fathers' tea, which they were sitting on a shitload of, and which was rotting in their warehouses. It was costing them a lot of money, and their wives were giving them a lot of grief about it.

So what they were trying to do now was to get the populace to revolt and kick the British out. Then everybody would have to buy their tea from the Founding Fathers at high Founding Father prices. Sam Adams admitted to me that it was a pretty complicated scam, but he felt it might work out. Especially if their new propaganda campaign equating expensive tea with freedom did its job. That explained the cries of: "They're trying to cheapen our tea!" and "We want expensive tea!" I had been hearing all over town.

I asked him how close we were to this Revolution of his. I didn't want to get caught up in it. I had to find Blinky. He said they were getting pretty close. Maybe another year. They were converting people to their cause, but it was slow going.

"It's hard to get people to understand that it's patriotic to be a traitor," Adams explained. "It's a difficult concept to understand, because it sounds so crazy when you first hear it. Then you slowly start to understand: Traitor=Patriot."

"The ones who get it right away are the ones who worry me," said Ben Franklin. "They understand things a little too easily, for my money. I mean, what if somebody comes along and tries to get them to 'understand' something about me? That I'm a lecherous old goat, or a British spy, or a penny-ante crook. See what I mean?"

There were murmurs of agreement among the other Founding Fathers about that. They had all been mistaken for penny-ante crooks at one time or another too.

Suddenly, the guy with the gold chains around

his neck who I'd run into back in the Old West entered the bar, spotted the Founding Fathers, compared their faces to some pictures in a book he had, then came over to introduce himself.

"F. Gordon Fantastic, Hollywood producer. Damn glad to meet you fellas. Now, I don't have a lot of time, so I want you all to listen up. First of all, I want you to wear these wristwatches from now on. And these five-corner hats." His assistant started handing these out. "And for God's sake stop talking with English accents."

"We're English," pointed out John Hancock.

"Talk with a twang," said Fantastic. "Through your nose and out of the side of your mouth. That's the way Americans talk. You want to sound like Americans, don't you? Bet your ass you do. Everybody does. Now, you, you're Washington, aren't you? Let's hear you say this line."

George Washington looked at the script Fantastic had handed him, then read the line: "I cannot tell a lie. F. Gordon Fantastic's new picture is 'Foundingfatheriffic'."

The producer pursed his lips and thought about the reading, then nodded. "Okay, not bad, but let's try it again. And this time try to look like you're telling the truth."

While Washington struggled with the line, Fantastic handed out more props for the Founding Fathers to wear, including goggles for Thomas Paine and vampire teeth for James Madison. At this point the bewildered Founding Fathers rebelled. They demanded to know why they should do any of these things he was suggesting. Fantastic said it was because they were destined to be great men, all of them, and it was important that they look and act like great men. They asked him what made him think they were going to be great men—this was the first they'd heard of it—and he tossed them the book he had been referring to. It was a U.S. history book that had been printed in the early 21st century. They began looking through it, and were soon thoroughly dazzled.

"Look at that!" said John Adams, awestruck. "I'm going to be the President!"

"Yeah," sneered George Washington, "The second President."

Fantastic pulled out some U.S. currency and postage stamps that had the Founding Fathers' likenesses on them and tossed them onto the bar.

"Here's more proof, if you need it."

The Founding Fathers stared at the wonderful money and beautiful stamps with amazement, saying things like: "It looks just like me, doesn't it?" and "Look how important I look!" and "My stamp is 14 cents, yours is only 12!"

"Who the hell is Andrew Jackson?" asked Franklin, holding up a twenty dollar bill, with a frown.

Fantastic took the bill and stuck it back in his pocket. "Never mind that one."

"Hey, how come I'm not on any of these?" asked Benedict Arnold, looking through them unhappily.

"I dunno," said Fantastic. "Maybe nobody likes you."

Arnold got a grim and thoughtful look on his face. "I see," he said.

This whole thing was a revelation to the Founding Fathers. Before, they had just thought of themselves as smugglers, rabble rousers, and petty swindlers. They didn't even call themselves the Founding Fathers. When they referred to themselves as a group at all it was as the "Boston Back Alley Boys, Plus Two". Now they suddenly began to think of themselves as Important Men. Men of Destiny.

Fantastic gave them a couple more props to add to their wardrobe, gave me a quizzical look— I think I reminded him of somebody. Me, probably—then said he had to go. He had to talk a guy named Cardigan into stopping the Charge of the Light Brigade mid-way through the Valley of Death to talk the whole charge over with his wife—make her understand how vital it was militarily, and how important charging was to a man, and get her okay on it. He said otherwise the Charge of the Light Brigade would only appeal to men. We pretended to know what he was talking about. And I think he respected us for that.

From that day forward the Founding Fathers became impossibly vain, strutting around town with their heads held so high they could hardly see where they were going, and riding around in their newly gilded carriages sneering down at the ordinary people, or being carried about in sedan chairs by those who were destined only to be Vice Presidents. John Adams was the worst snob, looking down his nose at everybody, and elbowing people out of the way, saying: "Out of my way, voter."

Paul Revere became so vain it ruined his business and cost him most of his friends. He stopped making silverware and crappy engravings and just spent his days walking around dreamily reciting Longfellow's poem: "Paul Revere's Ride"— which Fantastic had given him an advance copy of, 86 years before it was written—to anyone who would listen. He also somehow got the idea that everything he had to say (like "Lunch is coming.") was important, and had to be shouted over and over.

It was a glorious time for our Founding Fathers. They were having a blast. And so was I. Since I was a drinking buddy of theirs, they let me swagger around town with them. In return, I helped them out by shoving lesser people out of their way, so they could barrel on through. I did such a good job at this that they decided to make me a Junior Founding Father, and Washington said I could be in his cabinet. I said I was thinking of running for President myself. Then he could be in my cabinet. "Oh, you!" he said, and we started shoving each other playfully. When the fight was over we were friends again, but only after I promised to buy him some new teeth.

Because we were all having so much fun we

forgot about the things we should have been paying attention to. I totally forgot about Blinky. And the Founding Fathers began to neglect their Revolution. I have to take some of the blame for that. They kept starting to go out to inflame the masses a little, and remind everybody how bad the British were, and how expensive tea had to be if we were ever going to be free, but every time they started out the door of the tavern I'd say: "They'll still be gullible tomorrow. Have another drink." And they'd say: "Good thinking, Frank," and the party would start up again.

Because no one was pushing it anymore, interest in the Revolution started to fade. At the same time, the contamination from the future was starting to annoy everyone more than tea ever could. Not only were the people from 2010 taking all the best seats at the restaurants, and arguing about things nobody had ever heard of yet, and trying to sell everybody in town the Brooklyn Bridge, whatever that was, now they were starting to pollute Colonial culture with their 21st century ideas. They had started a campaign to stamp out snuff, due to the proven dangers, they said, of 2nd hand snuff—sneezing your snuff up somebody else's nose. A lot of Colonials liked snuff, and felt there was nothing wrong with having a nice relaxing sneeze now and then. This interference from the future had to stop, they felt. Never mind the British and their stupid tea, that whole thing never made a lot of sense anyway, let's rebel against this.

Of course, this sudden shift in public opinion alarmed the Founding Fathers when they heard about it. The Revolution against the British must happen! If America didn't gain its independence, there wouldn't be these wonderful ten-dollar bills and five-cent stamps. And the Founding Fathers' wives were already planning on how they were going to redecorate the United States. The Founding Fathers would be awfully unpopular at home if all this fell through now. I told them to stop worrying about it and let's have another drink, this one was on me, but they were genuinely alarmed now, and the party broke up for the first time in weeks.

The Founding Fathers hastily tried to whip up the Colonists into a frenzy about the British again with a new accusation: "The British are trying to sell us hot chocolate!" they said. "Evil... sticky...chocolaty... hot chocolate." But no one was even listening to them anymore. They were old news. The long planned Revolution against Britain was falling apart before it even got started, and a different Revolution was brewing.

The Founding Fathers made one last desperate try, holding a great meeting at Independence Hall where they presented their case for Revolution as forcibly as they could. The British, with their evil hot flavored drinks must be rebelled against at once. The people from the future were only a minor annoyance and could be dealt with, if necessary, in the future. I volunteered to speak at this rally to reassure everyone that the people of 2010 weren't the enemy. The real enemy was...

"Hi, I'm Frank Burly," I said, unthinkingly, as I bounded out onto the stage and prepared to give my speech.

There was immediately a great deal of grumbling from the audience, mixed with a few boos and hisses. The Founding Fathers didn't understand this, but I did. Uh-oh, I thought, I probably shouldn't have mentioned my name.

Nonetheless I plowed on, and started giving what I hoped history would record as "Burly's Great Speech"—the speech that brought the Colonials back to their senses and got the American Revolution back on track. A person likes to feel he's made his mark in the world, even if it's just a smear, so I welcomed this opportunity to speak. I started with a joke, which I had written myself. I tried to make it topical. "My Tory-in-law is so full of tea..." it began, but unfortunately, just when I got to the punch-line, which was: "Tea", I spotted Blinky in the crowd.

"You!" I yelled.

He took off, sneering at me back over his shoulder. I grabbed the Liberty Bell and threw it at him, cracking it. Then I took off after him, the rest of my great speech forgotten.

That was the last straw. Everybody in the Colonies had liked that Liberty Bell. It was a present from somebody, nobody remembered who, and I had busted it. The Colonists immediately rose up in Revolution—not against the British, like the Founding Fathers had always wanted, but against me and all the other troublemakers from the future. We had to be stopped before we did any more damage, like maybe sink the Liberty Boat, or run over the Liberty Dog.

The Founding Fathers did a quick about-face and tried to lead this new Revolution—they thought maybe they could salvage something out of this fiasco—but in the public's view they were forever linked with me now, and new leaders were chosen to lead the American Revolution. The old Founding Fathers were out.

The Colonial army chased me from Lexington to Ticonderoga to Brandywine to Saratoga. I really didn't stand much of a chance in any of these battles, there were too many of them and not enough of me, though I did manage to burn down New London, Connecticut. And I sank that Liberty Boat.

During my flight I wore a bright red coat, so I would blend in to my surroundings, which was probably a good idea, except my surroundings kept being the wrong color. The only time it worked was when I was standing in front of a firehouse, or in a pool of my own blood. Finally I ran to Yorktown where, due to a strategic mistake I still haven't figured out, I managed to corner myself and had to surrender.

I was brought back to Philadelphia in chains and taken to prison along with the rest of the people from the future, there to await our fate.

The Founding Fathers were pretty unhappy about the way things had turned out. They didn't strut around town anymore. They just sat gloomily around the bar all day, looking at the wonderful money and stamps with their faces on them that would never be legal tender now, and trying to sell each other tea.

"Paul Revere is here! Paul Revere is ready!" said Paul Revere, desperately.

"Put a sock in it, Revere," said Washington.

They took it hard, but it looked like I was about to take it harder.

CHAPTER TEN

"When are you getting hung?" asked the donut lady.

"Tomorrow," I said.

"Me too! Maybe we'll get hung from each other."

"That'd be nice, I guess."

We were in a cell together in a Colonial prison, along with hundreds of other people from 2010. It wasn't very comfortable. No beds. No chairs. You just had to sit on the floor in your own filth. And my filth, I noticed, was stupendous. But the lack of comfort didn't really matter too much because we weren't going to be there long enough for the pain to reach our brains anyway.

Prisons in those days were just places where they held you until they could figure out what to do with you. They already knew what they were going to do with me. They told me all about it. They were planning on hanging me, then beheading me, then tying a horse to each one of my arms and legs and having them run off in different directions, with a fifth horse jumping off a platform onto what was left. There was more, but I pretty much stopped listening after the fifth horse.

I saw one of the Founding Fathers outside the prison and called to him through the bars: "Hey, George! Get me out of here. Use your influence."

Washington glanced my way briefly, then went on sweeping the streets, acting as if he didn't know me. That made me mad. And after all I had done for him too.

Now that it was all over, and I had time to reflect on everything that had happened in the past months, I started to wonder what the hell it had all been about. It must have been about something, but damned if I could make sense of any of it.

I noticed F. Gordon Fantastic, the big Hollywood producer, sitting over in the corner making corrections on a pile of scripts. He had made the mistake of coming back to 1775 to give the Founding Fathers matching leather jackets to wear during the Revolution, and had gotten nabbed by the mob and tossed in here with the rest of us. I figured he might know what was going on. He had to know more than I did.

I got up and went over to him. He looked up at me with that same quizzical expression he had had before, then he finally recognized me and frowned.

"You're not wearing those lederhosen I gave you."

"Sorry."

"Sometimes I wonder why I bother."

"Uh huh. Well, like I said, I'm sorry. Say, do you know what all this is about?"

"What's what about?"

I made a sweeping motion, trying to describe, with that one motion, everything you've been reading about in this book. "This whole thing," I said. "Everybody going into the past, and all the garbage everywhere, and everybody in the history books acting screwy. You know..." I made the hand motion again. "...the whole thing."

He put down the script he'd been working on, thought for a moment, then said: "It all started with day-old donuts."

I sat down next to him. "Looks like I've come to the right guy. What do donuts have to do with any of this?"

"Plenty." He pointed. "You know her? Mrs. Donatelli?"

"The donut lady? Sure."

"Well, she was always complaining about having to sell day-old donuts for half price. They didn't cost her half price to make them. She thought it was a gyp."

"I know," I said. "She mentioned that to me too."

"She mentioned it to everybody. But she didn't know what to do about it. Then some high-powered efficiency expert from back East, Professor Blinkmaster of Blinkmaster Associates, showed up and offered to help her solve her problem. For a consideration, of course."

I held up the picture of Blinky. "This guy?"

He nodded. "That's the professor. Except he wore horn-rimmed glasses and had a beard that hooked around his ears. You know him?"

I nodded. "I've been chasing him throughout eternity."

"Sounds like you know him pretty well then. Anyway, he said what she needed was a way to take day-old donuts and sell them the day before, back when they were fresh and at the peak of their value. The only problem with that plan was that it was impossible under our current physical laws. But he said that physical laws were made to be broken."

"I've heard that saying."

"And if you had enough money you wouldn't have to obey any laws, physical or otherwise."

"I've heard the Kennedys can make themselves invisible."

He nodded. "The ordinary rules don't apply to them, because of their vast wealth."

"That's not fair," I pointed out.

"No," he agreed, "it's not fair." We shook hands on that. "So, anyway," he continued, "he talked her into raising a half a million dollars by issuing Donut Shop Bonds and speculative derivative financial instruments in the shape of donuts, and used the money, minus his hefty commission, of course, to build a machine that would open up a hole in the space/time continuum so old donuts could be sent back a day into the past where they could be sold as fresh.

"The finished machine worked perfectly, which surprised Mrs. Donatelli a little, the whole project had seemed a little far-fetched to her right from the beginning. And it surprised Professor Blinkmaster even more—which is confusing, because it was his idea in the first place. Anyway, once the machine was up and running she started secretly taking boxes of leftover donuts to the hole-in-time that the machine had created and sending them back to the previous day to be sold.

"She knew what she was doing wasn't quite on the up and up, she figured she had to be breaking some sort of law or regulation, so she tried to keep the whole thing quiet. But pretty soon people started finding out about it anyway. They'd notice her using it, or stumble onto it themselves, or she'd start blabbing about it to her customers before she could stop herself. You know how it goes."

I nodded. "I tried to keep quiet about something once..." I said, starting to tell my own story.

"Wonderful," said Fantastic, plowing ahead. "Anyway, everyone who found out about the hole started to blow the whistle on Mrs. Donatelli, but then they realized they could use the hole too. First other donut shops started using it. Then other kinds of businesses found they could use it to dispose of the useless part of their inventory—products that had become obsolete, outdated electronics, fad items, useless crap like that. If you sent the crap back far enough it would be new and exciting. You could make some money on it. At the very least you would have gotten it out of your warehouse. City Hall found it was a good place to dump votes they didn't want counted. The cops used it to quickly move up in rank. Environmentalists dumped all of the city's pollution down there for our parents and grandparents to deal with. And so on. Everybody knew what they were doing was pretty shady, if not downright illegal, so they kept their mouths shut about it. Officially, it wasn't happening."

"And you say everybody was in on it?"

"Everybody but you."

"I want to be in on it too."

"No. We don't need you."

"That's very short sighted."

"Perhaps. Then, as I understand it, some idiot broke into Mrs. Donatelli's donut shop in the middle of the night and started playing around with the machine, and ended up making a couple thousand more holes in time. Everybody fell into them, and pretty soon 2010 was empty, and everybody was down here. Made a mess of everything."

"Changing the subject," I said, quickly changing the subject, "what did you use the time tube for, Mr. Fantastic?"

He re-lit his cigar before he answered me. Then he looked at me shrewdly and said: "Who's the most misunderstood people in the world?"

I took a guess. "Hollywood producers?"

"That's right. Especially Hollywood producers with big cigars in their mouths."

"Like you."

"Yes. And why are we misunderstood?"

"Why?"

"Because the things we do don't make any sense, that's why. The stuff we put in our movies is all wrong. As a result, people misunderstand what we've done. See what I mean?"

"I suppose."

"See, the thing of it is, all producers have historical inaccuracies in their movies. It's hard to avoid them no matter how careful you are. And you wouldn't want movies to be completely accurate anyway. If you filmed the actual Civil War and showed it to audiences it would be five years long, and most of those five years would be boring. Just a lot of moving troops around and waiting for spring. It would be a yawnfest. The critics would trash it. So you've got to condense the action to make it appear more exciting than civil wars really are. That's the kind of thing producers have to worry about all the time. They have to make sure you get your money's worth at the theater, entertainment-wise, even if it means fudging the facts a little."

"It's good we've got producers looking out for us."

He nodded. "We're wonderful people, in our way. Now all that is if a producer is careful with the facts. Trying to do a good job, you know? But if you're not careful at all, like me, and if you make your movies really fast and cheap, and maybe your star is a comedian who likes to have a little fun with the facts, a lot of historical inaccuracies can begin to creep in. I guess I'm the champ at historically inaccurate pictures. And I've really had to take a lot of ribbing about it over the years. Got the horselaugh from everybody. I've even had grade school kids point at me and laugh."

"What did you do?"

"Well I didn't cry, if that's what you're thinking."

"What was so inaccurate about your pictures?"

"It varied. In one of my gladiator films, for example, I had Spartacus wearing wristwatches all up and down his arms and legs. Of course, they didn't have wristwatches back then. Everybody carried sundials or something."

"Oh, I see the inaccuracy there."

"So, when I found out about the time tube I came down here with some scripts and a few guys from our prop department and started fixing things up. I gave Spartacus some wristwatches and told him to wear 'em. I also gave him a derby hat and an 'I Like Ike' button. Don't know how those got into my picture. Mistake in the wardrobe department somewhere. But once the mistake was in the finished picture I had to make sure it was there in real life too."

"I see how it works now."

"Then I taught everybody in Biblical times to speak with a Brooklyn accent, so my bio-pic: "The

Unbelievable Story of Jesus" would seem more accurate. And I brought a couple of taxi cabs to the Battle of Gettysburg, so when Robert E. Lee hails one in one of my pictures and tells the driver to take him to Appomattox Court House, and U.S. Grant jumps in another one and says: 'Follow that cab!' audiences will stop pointing at that scene and saying: 'What the hell was that?'"

"You've had a lot to do down here."

"Never worked so hard in my life. But it was worth it. Now I'll get more respect for the films I've made. They might not be good, but at least they're accurate."

I suddenly remembered something. "You have gotten respect! I saw a statue of you on a horse back in 2010."

"No foolin'? On a horse?"

"Uh huh. And the inscription said: 'He told us how it was'."

This was the first time I'd ever seen F. Gordon Fantastic smile. He'd always looked vaguely irritated before. Or worried. Now he beamed. "Well, that's fine! That's all I've ever asked for, you know. Respect. Respect in the form of a statue of me on a horse. Oh, and money too. Respect and money."

"Sure."

"You've got to have money so you can afford to take a cab over to see your statue."

"Right."

"'He told us how it was!' Ain't that the truth!"

"It is now."

"Damn right." He puffed on his cigar with

pride. "Though, you know," he said, thoughtfully, "sometimes I wonder what this is all going to lead to, me changing history around willy-nilly like this. Then other times I wonder if my hair is on straight. You've got to have a sense of wonder in my business."

"Uh huh."

"But every time I question what I'm doing, I think: hey, whose movie is this? Then I go ahead and do whatever I want. The hell with the consequences. That's for my legal department to deal with."

I thought about everything he had been telling me. "I get the feeling I should kill you or something."

"Well don't do that."

"All right."

"Though I understand your point. A guy like me is kind of a menace. Did you know I have a big spider web in my office?"

"What do you use it for?"

He shrugged. "I just sit in it and kind of keep an eye on everything."

"Anything ever get caught in it?"

"The web?"

"Yeah."

"Sometimes. But nothing good, so far."

Fantastic broke off talking to me to chastise a guard who was slouching at his post. "Hey, Jack, either straighten up and try to look more like a guard or you're off of this picture."

"Huh?" said the guard.

"I want to feel like I'm being guarded by professionals here. The best of the best. I'm not feeling that. You can be replaced, you know."

"It is not for the prisoners to determine the posture..."

Fantastic flipped open his cell phone and barked into it: "Get me Central Casting."

The guard instantly straightened up.

Fantastic eyed him for a moment, then seemed satisfied. I liked the new look better too. I really felt like I was being guarded now.

I stood up. "Well, thanks for all the information, Mr. Fantastic. Explaining the plot to me and everything."

"My pleasure."

I pulled out the picture of Blinky and showed it to him again. "If you happen to see this guy anywhere, let me know."

He glanced at the picture, then pointed. "There he is. In the cell next to ours, with his ear hanging out, listening to us."

I looked. It was Blinky, all right. I hadn't recognized him before because with his ear hanging out he looked like a completely different guy.

"You!" I yelled.

I ran to the bars separating the cells and tried to grab Blinky through them, while he taunted me, and the guards whacked both of us with clubs to get us to settle down.

While I was still trying to reach Blinky—I couldn't quite do it, but I almost could. If only I could make my arms just a little longer... yes, they were starting to get longer now, I was sure of it... just another five feet more—there was a sudden disturbance outside the prison. The guards stopped hitting us and ran to the window.

Cavemen, Roman gladiators, ancient Egyptians, and all sorts of other people from other time periods had gathered outside the prison and were demanding that "Frank Burly" be handed over to them. There was even an old woman from Massachusetts with a wart on her nose writing out the demand in the sky.

Evidently the people in the other eras I'd visited hadn't been satisfied with just running me off. They wanted to get me and tear me into a thousand pieces. One piece for each of them. Some of them had followed me into the time tube and had only just now caught up to me. The word was spreading throughout time that this was where I was, and more people from more time periods were showing up every minute, clustering around the prison and demanding in a thousand different Brooklyn accents that I be handed over to them.

The prison guards, of course, didn't like people telling them what to do with their prisoners. Especially not riff-raff from other eras. The residents of the Colonial Period had had it up to here with people from other eras. So the guards told the cavemen and the Romans and all the rest of them to piss off. Just piss off, that's all.

After the guards had been told to say that

again, and they had said it again with knobs on, the fight started. It didn't last too long. The guards were pretty badly outnumbered already, and more Vikings and Transcendentalists were showing up every minute. Finally the guards were overwhelmed, and a battering ram was used to punch a hole in the wall.

Immediately, Blinky ran out through the hole, followed by me. The rest of the prisoners were right behind us, followed by more guards. The people from other eras, who had been momentarily caught back on their heels by the suddenness of it all, let out a howl of rage and lit out after us.

News of the spectacular jailbreak spread quickly through town and everybody dropped what they were doing and joined the chase. Then other towns started hearing about it.

Blinky got to the time tube first. He jumped in and headed up towards the future, taunting me over his shoulder. I followed, taunting the people behind me, which by this point included just about everyone from 1775, and a lot more besides.

I caught up to Blinky just before he reached the top of the time tube.

"Gotcha, you little bastard!"

I grabbed him by the scruff of his neck, gave him a triumphant shake, then extracted my stolen ID from his pocket, and put it back in my pocket where it belonged. Then I got back my hat, which he had been wearing all this time. It was a rare moment of triumph for me. I'd finally caught the man I'd been hired to find, and I'd also recovered my precious precious identity. It was another happy ending to another exciting Frank Burly Adventure.

"Gotcha, you big bastard!" the million people behind me said.

As two million hands went around my neck and started to squeeze, our momentum carried us to the end of the time tube, the top of the tube burst open, and we all began spilling out into 2010.

CHAPTER ELEVEN

We crashed back into the present and landed on the sidewalk not far from the donut shop just at the moment when Mrs. Donatelli was taking her first box of day-old donuts to drop down the hole. When she saw us she hurriedly went back into her shop and peered at us through the window.

Blinky had gotten jarred loose from my grasp when we hit the ground. I made a grab for him, but before I could catch him and beat the hell out of him, everybody started beating the hell out of me. Beat the shit out of me too.

After awhile somebody said: "Okay, that's enough, he's dead", but since it was me that had said it, everybody just kept hitting me. They didn't even slow down. Finally somebody said: "All right, he's really dead now" (me again), and they stopped hitting me and left me lying there in a heap.

When I was pretty sure they were gone—the garbage people were there now, trying to get me into their truck—I slowly picked myself up and checked myself out for injuries. I had 1406 of them, three short of my record. I thought of calling the mob back, but decided against it.

I looked around for Blinky. I couldn't see him, but what I did see amazed me. I had always said that the changes people were making back in the past might end up screwing up the present—you heard me say it. You're a witness—and now here was the proof right before my eyes that I was completely and utterly wrong.

The year 2010 was different all right. But different better. There were palm trees everywhere. Swimming pools. Fabulous mansions. People were riding around in limousines and fancy sports cars. All the women were beautiful, and all the men were strong. I felt like I had walked right into the middle of a motion picture. And a pretty darn good motion picture, by the looks of it.

It just shows how a few changes here and there, over thousands of years, can have a huge cumulative effect. Just by altering our history a little bit to make it be more in line with Hollywood's view of things, to give everything more of a Hollywood sensibility, our society had gradually evolved into a totally Hollywood World. A world where everybody was a star, nothing lasted for more than 132 minutes, and everything looked like a million bucks.

It wasn't a perfect world, of course. Everybody's dialogue stunk, for example. And there were continuity problems. You'd be talking to somebody on the veranda and then suddenly they'd be in the swimming pool. Then they'd be back on the veranda, but you wouldn't have met them yet. There were big lizards everywhere too—that was a change that wasn't necessarily for the better, and I didn't see what it had to do with the movies—but they didn't seem to be bothering anybody. So, like I said, there were problems with this new version of 2010, there were things you could criticize about it, but overall it was pretty great.

As I was marveling at all the improvements, I happened by the park where F. Gordon Fantastic's statue was, and saw him standing there gazing up at it, and reading the inscription with delight.

"'He told us how it was.' Say, that's nice." He turned to me. "Looks great, doesn't it? I think the artist has really captured my jowls."

I shrugged. "It looks okay, I guess. All jowls look pretty much the same to me." Suddenly I noticed something. "Hey, is that a statue of me over there?"

Another large statue had been erected near the one of F. Gordon Fantastic. It looked kind of like me—certainly the clothes and the hat were the same—but the face was kind of vague. Could have been anybody, really. And it somehow managed to look both heroic and sinister at the same time. The inscription on the base of the statue said: "Frank Burly: He Did It All".

I frowned. "I don't remember 'Doing It All'. I think they've mistaken me for somebody else."

"They've mistaken you for everybody else. You're forgetting the plot of this picture."

"What picture?"

"The main theme here, as I see it, is Man's Struggle To Maintain His Identity In A Changing World."

"Is it?"

He nodded. "In a word: Identity theft. That's been your driving motivation all along, even though you keep forgetting it."

"Oh, yeah, that's right." I checked my pocket. It was empty. Blinky had lifted my ID again.

"Practically everybody in history is using your name now. Everybody's got your ID except you."

He opened up his wallet and showed me a driver's license with his picture and my name on it. "See there?"

"Hey, can I have that?" I asked.

"No," he said, putting his wallet away. "I might need it for something. So every time anybody does anything anywhere, it looks like you did it. It's a great deal for you, really. Everybody else does all the work, all you have to do is pose for the statues and the wanted posters."

"I suppose you're right."

"I 'tell us how it was'," he said, indicating the inscription on his statue. Then he looked closer at the two statues, comparing them. "I think your statue is bigger than mine." He sounded worried.

I looked at the statues. "It is, a little, unless you count your horse's tail."

He stared at the statues for a long moment, considering. Finally he said: "I think I'm going to count the tail."

"Okay."

I left him there admiring his statue, and reading the inscription over and over, using different inflections each time to see which way sounded best.

I told you the world of 2010 was a paradise—with, okay, maybe a few small problems here and there—but it was becoming less of a paradise every second. It was being flooded with people. People were pouring out of the time tube from the past like water out of a faucet—not just from 1775, but from all historical eras. It was like all of the people who had ever lived were being blown out onto the street at this one point in time. A scientist told me that he thought that so many people leaving the past at the same time had caused a vacuum to be formed somehow, and now everybody from history was being sucked through to 2010, whether they wanted to come or not. I asked him how long it would take him to fix all that. He said he couldn't fix it. I told him he was fired. He said I couldn't fire him, he quit.

The people who lived in 2010 complained bitterly about their paradise being trashed up like this—expressing themselves loudly in the badly written movie dialogue they'd been taught to speak from birth: "Dude!" "Not!" "Noooo!" and

"Wassup?" They weren't expressing their feelings clearly, but we could tell what they meant by their over-the-top gestures, outrageous eye-rolling, and gratuitous nudity. They didn't like it. That much was plain. And I couldn't really blame them.

One of the Colonials I knew from 1775—we had shot each other off Bunker Hill—walked up to me and indicated the crowded landscape with disgust. "And you were bad-mouthing our time period! This is terrible."

I frowned. I don't like outsiders criticizing my time period. I don't know why. I just don't. "It was all right until you got here," I said.

"Maybe so, but it stinks now."

"Yeah, but maybe the stink is coming from you. That's what I'm saying."

"It's not though!" he said.

"Yeah, but how do we know that?"

"You'll just have to take my word for it!"

"That's not good enough!"

"It will have to be good enough for now!"

"Well it isn't!"

We argued a little more like that, back and forth, one great line after another, until the argument finally ended with us knocking each other down. But once he had left and I had calmed down a little bit I had to admit to myself that he was right. The 21st century certainly wasn't looking its best at the moment. It was far too crowded. And more people were spewing out of the time tube every few seconds. They came out in bursts, usually making a tuba sound for some reason. It wasn't long before Central City was twelve people deep everywhere you looked. It was awful. You could hardly move. Especially if you were in the middle of the pile, like I was. And the lines at the theaters were ridiculous. I finally stopped going to the theater entirely.

Nobody seemed to be trying to do anything about the problem. They were just standing there complaining about it. So that's what I did too. I blamed the Democrats, of course. But I also blamed the Republicans. Because I wasn't sure which party was in power at the moment. So I just let everybody have it.

It was while my complaints were at their loudest and most contradictory that I heard a voice from somewhere down near the first layer of people.

"Hot dogs! Get your hot dogs!"

Along with everyone else, I started looking around for the hot dog guy. There was a lot of movement in the pile as everyone looked for the source of the cries. Suddenly the cries stopped.

After a long pause another voice said: "Ladies and gentlemen, the hot dog guy is dead."

Now things were really getting bad. Now we were out of hot dogs too. And more people kept arriving from the past every second. Soon Central City was twenty people deep. Then fifty. It was beginning to look like the dire warnings of the scientists about overpopulation—the warnings that mankind had ignored for so long, with such great success—were starting to come true.

As the flood of people into 2010 increased, the opening in the time tube widened and entire time periods started squeezing out. I almost got hit on the head by Revolutionary France, if you can believe it. Then, as if in an attempt to top that, the Paleozoic Era spewed out of the tube, ran into the Roaring 20's, fell over, and killed a guy. It's true. I saw it. Crushed his larynx, I think.

Of course a situation like that can't go on forever—you wouldn't want it to—so finally the Earth became so crowded and top heavy that it became destabilized and started wobbling with increasing violence on its axis.

This caused everyone to be violently thrown around in all directions. Buildings were ripped out by their roots and sent flying through the air. Mountains, too. And leaves, of course. Everything was flying through the air. I flew about a mile and a half myself, finally landing at an airport, which was a bit of luck, except I got stuck in the side of a plane, and ended up in a big argument with a stewardess.

Scientists were running around urgently warning everyone of the possible dangers of all this. Flying mountains could damage the environment, they said. Even worse, they could damage a scientist. We had to do something before—but it was already too late.

Suddenly the Earth stopped completely, jerking to a stop so violently that it threw us all over the place one last exciting time, with a lot of people screaming in terror, and the rest of us yelling: "whee!"

Then the Earth exploded, sending everyone, including yours truly, flipping end over end out into space.

"Whew," I thought, as I spun crazily into the void, "I'm glad that's over."

CHAPTER TWELVE

When I regained consciousness, I found that I was floating in space surrounded by a small cocoon of atmosphere that had been blown off the planet with me. It was held in place by my personal gravitational pull, I guess. Or maybe my smell. I don't know. What holds cocoons of atmosphere in place? Do you know? I tried to ask a nearby scientist about it, but he was dead.

There was a lot of debris from the exploded Earth around me. And there were a lot of people, too. Many of them had cocoons of atmosphere around them, like I did. Many more had no cocoons. I found myself being envious of people with bigger cocoons—some of them were having a party in there—and couldn't help but point and laugh at the people who had smaller cocoons than I did, or no cocoon at all. Ha ha, I thought, small or no cocoon.

Some of the people didn't seem to know what had happened to them. I saw one man watering a small patch of lawn that had been blown off the

Earth with him. The water had stopped and he couldn't figure out why. He kept looking in the nozzle. I had to laugh at that. He didn't know what was going on! Ha ha ha ha ha. I was having a lot of fun up here. Outer space was a million laughs today.

I saw the donut lady drift by. For a few moments her cocoon came into contact with mine and we could talk to each other. She seemed a little despondent about the way things had turned out.

"If I'd known this would happen," she said, shaking her head, "I would have just thrown those day-old donuts away."

"Well, don't do that."

A donut sounded good right then.

As I floated on, one cheerful thought struck me. Now I truly was The Last Detective Alive. Now, finally, all those business cards I had printed up were right. Just as I thought that, a cocoon full of detectives floated by. Must have been a hundred of them in there. It looked like they were having some kind of a convention, judging by the signs and banners and all the speeches being made. I frowned and put my business cards back in my pocket.

Then I began to notice something was wrong. I seemed to be running out of air, if the color (bright blue) and shape (funny shape) of my face was any indication. And isn't my chest supposed to be going in and out? Mine's just sitting there. I figured I'd better do something about this quick.

I'd better think of a plan—one that would get me out of this mess and fix everything back up the way it used to be. And maybe make me some money too. And fix it so I'm better looking. I knew it was going to have to be a pretty darn good plan to do all that. And, I'd better think of it in less than nine minutes, because that was about all the time I had left.

I managed to come up with a plan in just under eight minutes, but after I had examined it from every angle I realized it wasn't workable in this situation. It required powerful machinery, thousands of experts, a time paradox, a nuclear submarine, a cat, a crowbar, and a birthday cake. And all I had was a mouthful of air and a bad idea. I reluctantly abandoned my plan. But even though I only had a minute left, I didn't give up. Where there's life, there's hope. I forget who said that. Tall guy. He's dead now. Anyway, I got to work on a new plan—a plan I would call Plan B. This plan would have to be a lot simpler, and much worse than the other one, because I didn't have a lot of time left to work on it.

Just before I used the last of my air to yell at some teenagers who were making a lot of noise while some of us in space were trying to think, I found myself drifting down towards a small asteroid. I immediately abandoned my work on Plan B. This was my Plan B now, I decided. And it was working. It was working beautifully.

The asteroid didn't have a whole lot of gravity, but it had enough to bloody my nose when I hit it. And it had a small but potent atmosphere of breathable oxygen, so I could, and did, yell at those teenagers now.

While I was getting in a last word to the teens, reminding them to stay in school and do what their mother says, an old gent with white hair shuffled up to me.

"Welcome," he said.

"Who are you?" I asked. "And what is this place?"

He pointed at a sign. "Read the sign, stupid. It's heaven."

I looked at the sign. It said "Heven."

"You spelled it wrong," I said.

"What's that?"

"There's supposed to be an 'a' in there someplace."

He looked at the sign for a moment and scratched his head. Finally he turned back to me. "You want to come in here or not?"

"I dunno." I looked up into the blackness of space. I certainly didn't want to go back up there. But I wasn't sure I wanted to commit myself to this place either. I decided to play it cagey. "Maybe."

"Have you been good?"

"What's it to you?"

"I was just curious."

"Well mind your own business from now on."

"All right. Hey, are you coming in? I can't stand out here talking all day. I'm a busy man."

"You don't look very busy."

"No," he admitted. "That's just something I say to get people to hurry up."

I looked through the gates into 'Heven'. "What's the catch?" I asked. "If I come in do I have to praise you or something?"

"Well, you don't have to, but I'd certainly appreciate it. You do have to put up with my wife's cooking. That's kind of a catch. And there's the ten bucks to get in. Eight bucks if you have one of our coupons."

"Coupons?"

"Merchandising gimmick. We put them in the backs of Bibles. Gets you two dollars off."

"Well I don't have a coupon."

"Then it's the full ten dollars."

I hesitated. Ten dollars was a lot of money. I only had a hundred and ninety.

"Why don't you come in and have a look around?" he suggested. "Then you can decide."

"All right."

He swung open the Pearly Gates and I followed him in.

The place didn't look like much to me. "This kind of looks like an amusement park," I said, looking around. There were cheap roller coasters, souvenir shops where you could buy T-shirts with some of the funnier Bible verses on them, and a couple of those crooked halo-toss games. "And not a very good amusement park, at that," I added.

"I had to do a lot of it on the cheap," he admitted. "But it's the idea of the thing that's important. That's the big selling point—what the place is, not what it looks like. Heaven is the most pre-sold concept there is. Everyone is expecting there to be such a place, and everyone wants to go there. So I set one up."

"I understand the scam, but how do you make a living doing this out here? This place is pretty remote. And you don't seem to have a lot of customers so far. How do you show a profit?"

"Well, I don't, yet."

"So how do you keep operating?"

"My wife's got some money." He indicated a big bucket of something. "You want to answer some prayers while you're here?"

"Nah."

I looked the rest of the place over. It got cheesier the farther away from the Pearly Gates you got. I saw some angels sleeping in the streets, and a lot of empty beer bottles. A couple of the angels approached me for money with hard luck stories I didn't bother to listen to. The old man could tell I wasn't too impressed. He seemed a little embarrassed.

"I know it doesn't look like much now," the old man said, "but me and my new assistant over there are coming up with some great ideas to spiff the place up."

He pointed at his new assistant, who was putting up a sign that said: "Nude" something. It was Blinky.

"You!" I yelled.

He threw down the sign and took off running.

I followed, yelling words that probably hadn't been heard in heaven for years.

I chased him all through heaven—up and down the roller coasters, through the Haunted House, where Holy Ghosts kept jumping out at us, and past the arcade where a guy who looked like Jesus tried to guess our sins. Then I finally got him cornered between a couple of harps. With no place to go but up, he sprang into the air. Since the asteroid didn't have much in the way of gravity, he managed to make it all the way out into space in one bound. I followed, remembering to take an extra big mouthful of air before I jumped. You need air to live in outer space. We know that now.

The old man unhappily watched us disappear into space. There went a couple of customers, he was probably thinking. The last I saw of him he was looking at his "Heven" sign and scratching his head again. I'm sure there was supposed to be an "a" in there someplace. I really think I was right about that.

I don't know if it's because I got a better jump off the asteroid, or just because I've had a lot more experience in outer space than most people, but I caught up to Blinky pretty easily.

"Gotcha!" I said, grabbing him by the neck.

"Hey, lemme go," he complained.

"Oh no you don't," I said, grimly. I wasn't falling for that one again.

Keeping a firm grip on his neck, I took a look around to see what to do next. We were floating unprotected in open space, with two faces full of air, so whatever we did next, it was important that it be done quickly, and that it be a lot different in every way from what we were doing now.

My first idea was to go farther out into space where I could think. Maybe lie down for awhile out there and get some sleep. I'd think better if I had some sleep. Then I thought maybe it might be a better idea to try to get back to that asteroid—that place with all the air. Of course there was the ten dollar admission fee to be considered there, whereas the place where I was was free. From a financial standpoint I was better off here. From an oxygen standpoint, the asteroid was better. I pulled a coin out of my pocket and got ready to flip it. Heads—ten dollars. Tails—air. But then I suddenly noticed that I didn't have to make a decision about where to go next. The decision was being made for me.

Blinky and I were slowly drifting down towards a small planet. Some of the other people from the exploded Earth were floating that way too. Still others were floating off into deep space or in towards the sun. I saw a number of the ones heading for the sun put on sunglasses. Some people are always prepared.

I counted myself as one of the lucky ones until I saw what was happening to people when they entered the planet's atmosphere. They all started burning up because of the friction. I didn't want that to happen to me. What I needed, I decided, was a heat shield. So when we began entering the atmosphere I held Blinky up in front of me to take the brunt of the heat.

"Look, Blinky," I said enthusiastically, "It's a planet!"

It worked for awhile, I think he liked having a front row seat, but then he realized what I was doing and somehow managed to switch places with me. Now he was holding me up to see the nice planet, and I was taking all the heat. I frowned and switched us back. We alternated back and forth like that all the way through the atmosphere until we splashed down into what I thought was somebody's backyard swimming pool, but which turned out to be a very small ocean.

I had noticed during re-entry that the planet we were heading towards looked exactly like the Earth, just on a smaller scale. And that's exactly what it turned out to be. When Blinky and I sputtered our way out of the ocean and got to shore, I saw a sign that said: "Welcome To Parallel Earth 7, Your Home Away From Home".

I must say I think I prefer the old original Earth. This one was only 80 miles in diameter. You could jump across the Atlantic, which was about the size of a small creek. Everybody had Frenchmen looking in their windows. And only three people could fit in the Empire State Building at any one time. My statue was smaller here too, though it was still a little bigger than Fantastic's (that tail doesn't count). Everything on the planet was smaller. And smaller isn't always better, no matter what the small guys will tell you.

The other refugees from the original Earth (you could tell which ones they were because their faces were scorched from re-entering the atmosphere without a heat shield) weren't too happy with the smallness of this place either, but nobody disliked it enough to turn around and jump back into space to die. This was good enough, everybody decided. We'd stay here.

I went home, dragging a squirming Blinky along with me, kicked the Parallel Me out of the house (he was smaller than I was so that was no problem), then changed, showered, and prepared my bill for Parallel Mr. Acropolis. It was going to be a big one. I had done a lot of work for him, over countless centuries of time. He owed me plenty for all this.

CHAPTER THIRTEEN

I dragged Blinky over to Mr. Acropolis' house and banged on the doorbell with his head. The house looked different to me, I noticed, as I banged away, whistling along with the doorbell. I couldn't put my finger on what was different at first, then I realized that it was a lot smaller, just like everything else was on this planet. It was still impressive though. The doorknob was as big as twenty doorknobs. I started banging Blinky's head on that

When we were finally admitted, I dragged Blinky in to Acropolis' study and threw him down in front of the desk.

"Well, here he is. I've got your man for you," Blinky said, pretending he was me again.

"Quiet, Burly," I said, getting confused myself for a minute there.

Acropolis was looking back and forth at us, frowning. He had his finger poised over the button that made servants fall out of the ceiling.

"I've got your man for you, Mr. Acropolis," I

said, glaring at Blinky for stealing my line. I pulled out my expense book and consulted it. "Let's see... that will be... um... three billion years...two hundred dollars a day... four cents a mile...suit laundering (once)... gratuity to insure promptness... value added tax (in U.K. only)... comes to a total of... eight hundred and sixty three hundred million billion thousand million thousand dollars."

"Ridiculous!" exclaimed Acropolis. "There is no such amount of money."

I was suddenly unsure of my facts. "Is there a thousand dollars?"

"Yes, but I won't pay even that."

"But..." I held out the expense book.

"Why should I pay you to apprehend a man who has done me such a valuable service? He put me onto a good thing. My President Snodwell autographs are worth a fortune. Much more than I paid for them."

Blinky was aghast. "They are?"

"Oh, yes. He was a hero of the Revolution, and the first President, as you told me. I've done a lot of research since you arranged for me to buy my collection. I've even read Snodwell's autobiography: 'Grocer To Glory', and how you could get his autograph for me so cheaply, I don't know. Nearly all the other autographed material you recommended has made me a handsome profit too. The hoofprints of General Donkey still aren't worth anything," he frowned a little at this, "but my other winnings more than offset my losses on those."

"Hey, wait a minute," said Blinky, "Snodgrass wasn't the first U.S. President."

Acropolis frowned. "Of course he was. Everyone knows that. You're the one who told me about him."

"What about George Washington?"

"The street sweeper? What has he got to do with this?"

Blinky looked at me, confused.

"It's a long story," I said. "Want to hear it?"

"No." He turned back to Acropolis. "Hey, I'm beginning to think I want those autographs back, Mr. Acropolis."

"And while you're giving him back his autographs," I said, "how about paying me my money?" I consulted my expense book again. "Eight hundred and sixty three hundred million..."

As Blinky and I picked ourselves up off the pavement in front of the Acropolis mansion, after bouncing off the mansion across the street, we looked at each other in dismay. Blinky felt like he'd been cheated somehow. And I felt like I'd been cheated in a very specific way.

"Well, that was a washout," I said. "Three billion years work for nothing."

"You said it," agreed Blinky. "Well, so long, Burly."

He started to leave, but couldn't because I was still holding on to the scruff of his neck.

"Hey, let go of my scruff."

But I wasn't letting Blinky go. Not after all I'd gone through to catch him. Maybe nobody else wanted him, but I did.

Ignoring his protests, I dragged him back to my house and locked him up in my basement.

I kept him down there for a couple of weeks, ignoring his pleading, and his threats, and rejecting his ideas for improving the basement. They were probably good ideas, but I just didn't have the money to make any extensive renovations right then. Why couldn't he understand that?

I probably would have kept him down there forever—it wasn't costing me anything, I didn't have to feed him—but the neighbors started noticing the smell. And the cops started nosing around and asking me what I had down there that was making all the noise. I managed to get them to go away by saying: "Probably nothing", but they came back the very same day saying: "What do you mean 'probably'?" It finally got to the point where I was forced to choose—either get Blinky out of my basement, or put the cops down there too. I reluctantly decided to let Blinky go. He immediately ran off, taunting me. I didn't bother to follow. I'd had enough.

So that's the story. That's how I captured the notorious conman and identity thief Edward Blinkman, alias Blinky, alias Professor Blinkmaster, alias Frank Burly etc. It's also how I became The Last Detective Alive, which I still insist on billing myself as. I don't care how many detectives there are in town, or how many you personally have seen today. I didn't have all those business cards printed up just to throw them away. I'd rather be wrong than lose money any day.

The case wasn't a total success from every angle. Like I said, I didn't get paid. And the doctors say some of these head injuries of mine are fatal. And some people still implicate me in the destruction of the original Earth. They say it was all my fault. The truth is, it was only partly my fault. Look it up. There was some talk for awhile about a government investigation into the whole thing, and I had my bags packed, because all government investigations always seem to lead to me. But in the end the whole case got lost in the shuffle somehow and was forgotten. I was relieved by that, but not surprised. That's the reason governments are inefficient. To protect people like me.

I probably should have made a lot of money out of all this because Frank Burly autographs are worth a fortune now. If you believe the history books, Frank Burly did everything. So his autograph is worth everything. All advanced collectors these days know that a Frank Burly autograph is the cornerstone of any fine autograph collection. Unfortunately every time I sign my name people say it's a forgery. That's not the way Frank Burly signs his name, they tell me. Try again. And I do try again, but they still don't like it. The "Frank" looks all right, I'm told, no problem there, but the "Burly" is a dead giveaway. So not only do I not get any money, I usually have to spend some time in jail. So I've pretty much stopped signing autographs now.

The only other complaint I have is that donuts are smaller on this parallel Earth. So I end up having to buy twice as many to get just as full. I'm only getting half as much for my donut dollar. So the whole thing ended up costing me money. That's life, I guess. It's my life, anyway.